CRUSHED TO DEATH

From less than two yards away, Rourke looked at the man—he was at least seven feet tall. The technician's body looked to have been poured into the fatigue uniform with his muscles rippling visibly underneath it.

"Vitamins?" Rourke asked him.

The technician smiled, hurling himself forward. John Rourke side-stepped. But he couldn't get out of the reach of the huge man's fists. He took a glancing blow and edged back—and then Rourke stepped in and hit the technician with a right hook to the chin. The big man toppled over . . . right on top of Rourke!

The next split second was critical. The technician had the bulk and strength to pin Rourke down and kill him. And Rourke wasn't sure if he had it within himself to survive. . . .

THE SURVIVALIST SERIES
by Jerry Ahern

#11

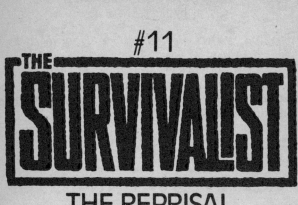

THE REPRISAL
BY JERRY AHERN

ZEBRA BOOKS
KENSINGTON PUBLISHING CORP.

Any resemblance to persons, governments, businesses, governmental entities living, dead, or operating or having operated is purely coincidental.

ZEBRA BOOKS

are published by

Kensington Publishing Corp.
475 Park Avenue South
New York, N.Y. 10016

Copyright © 1985 by Jerry Ahern

Third printing: February 1988

Printed in the United States of America

For Don Tope, who kept coming up with solutions — well, here it really is, my friend.

Chapter One

He opened his eyes. He closed them again — the bluish light hurt. After a moment he tried opening his eyes again, craning his neck — stiff. It was another dream. But his neck really — his eyes were really open. He looked upward, studying the small panel to his right. "Elapsed time," the small, stenciled words said. He squinted his eyes shut. There was a digital readout over the stenciled words — he'd seen it, remembered that it should have been there. But he had not read it. He tried to do that; his eyes open again, squinting at it: "Years — 501; Month — 3; Days — 3; Hours — 14; Minutes — 6; Seconds — 19." It changed to twenty just as he blinked.

"My God — it really happened." But his voice was so hoarse, so dry, that he barely recognized it.

He stretched himself as he climbed from the chamber, the lid fully risen in perfect synchronicity with his body as he had finally sat up. He had swung his legs — with difficulty and slowly — and now sat on the small shelflike seat at the outside edge of the chamber, his arms and shoulders and legs and neck stiff, aching dully. His stomach felt so terribly empty. He noticed inside the panel a plastic-covered printed sheet. He squinted to read it. "Important — read this thoroughly before attempting any movement after awakening from cryogenic sleep." He skimmed to the bottom of

7

the plastic-coated advisory. Under his breath, just to hear his own voice, he read: "For detailed information consult TM-86-2-21 located beneath the shelf to the left of the cryogenic chamber."

He shrugged — he hurt. He sat there, looking about the main cabin.

Some of the lights on the flight control panels were out — he could tell that from the distance. At the top center of the panel, the small computer display three was out. He stared around him then — there was a second chamber near him.

The lid was rising, the man inside it rising, like someone rising from a coffin, and for a moment his childhood fears given form and substance by horror films of Bela Lugosi seized him. He tried to stand up, to look inside. He shook his head — dizziness. He watched as the lid of the cryogenic chamber raised to a fully open position.

His voice still hoarse, hard to talk with, he said, "Craig — hey — hey, Craig — Craig Lerner — hey — it happened. Like it said in the orders — they could recall us. But they didn't recall us — it happened — Christ — it happened."

Craig Lerner turned his face to look at him. "It happened, Craig — World War Three — Holy Jesus — " He closed his — it looked to him like Craig Lerner was starting to sob, but there weren't any tears.

It had been more than an hour — he checked another of the elapsed time indicators located throughout the flight deck of the shuttle. But he could walk, albeit stiffly. Flight Officer Craig Lerner beside him, he stopped beside one of the viewing ports into the cargo hold. He pressed a button, surprised that the covering for the viewing port still worked. Like a flower unfolding, the viewing port cover peeled from the center to the sides, the view through the port now quite clear. He pressed his forehead against the plexiglass, leaning hard against it, the absence of gravity making him very ill suddenly. Twenty cryogenic chambers identical to the one he had left. Smaller chambers holding embryonic animals and other living things. Packing containers—holding he didn't even fully remember what.

He leaned back from the viewing port and held to the handrail along the fuselage.

"Do we wake 'em up, captain?"

"What's this captain shit—after five centuries you gotta call me Captain—"

"Do we wake 'em up, Tim?"

"No—just the science officer—the twenty in there stay put. We only wake 'em up if there's something down there—if, ahh—then otherwise, ahh—" He didn't finish the sentence. "You go wake up—ahh—"

"Jeff? Jeff Styles?"

"Yeah—shit," and Timothy Dodd shook his head to clear it. "I can't remember a damn thing—gotta sit down a while."

"It's all right, Tim."

He looked after Lerner as Lerner started across the flight deck toward the third cryogenic chamber there, the only one unopened. He shook his head—if there was something down there, then the rest—then the rest . . .

Walking along the handrail to guide himself, he had reached the pilot's seat and slumped into it, strapping himself down to try and get rid of the floating feeling inside his stomach and after a time the feeling had

9

eased. Lerner seemed to be getting along much better, and Dodd wondered if it were a function of age. Lerner was thirty-three and he, Dodd, was forty-four. He shrugged, but only a little, remembering he did not want to move his body more than needed.

He had not opened the viewport — not yet. He had read the copy of TM-86-2-1 — Lerner had brought it to him. It advised against eating or drinking for several hours after awakening, alerted the awakening sleeper that gastric distress, diarrhea, and nausea might well accompany initial eating and drinking. He shook his head — the thought of nausea made him nauseous. But he fought to control that — after five hundred years, there could be nothing left to throw up. He had seen his face reflected in the viewport plexiglass when he had looked to the twenty sleepers he carried as his main, his most precious cargo. He had what looked like two or three weeks' worth of a beard. He had lost weight in his face. And as he had strapped himself into his pilot's seat, his hands had felt weak, clumsy, his fingers stiff. TM-86-2-1 indicated this would be a likely reaction.

Lerner — he heard Lerner's voice, turned too fast to look at Lerner and, feeling the nausea, closed his eyes against it.

"Captain — I got Styles awake — he's feelin' shitty — like you. But we'll have him up — "

There was an air-sick bag and Timothy Dodd fitted it over his mouth and nose, made the seal so nothing would escape and retched into it — but nothing came up.

Lerner sat in the copilot's seat to his right, Styles behind them, Dodd's and Lerner's chairs cranked toward Styles so they could talk. Styles seemed well enough now. "I can't believe this is happening—I mean—have either of you considered this may be a dream—perhaps a common dream?"

"You don't throw up in a dream," Dodd told him. "You're the science officer—what the hell is it with this dream crap?"

"It was just a suggestion." Styles nodded, holding his palms outward to them like shields. "There's a school of philosophy that held that reality was possibly a fantasy and that all of life experiences were simply manufactured in the mind—"

"That kinda crap could drive ya nuts just thinking about it—especially up here, in a situation like this. Hell—there's never been a situation like this."

"Tim is right, Jeff—if this is all a dream, it sure as hell seems realistic enough to me." Dodd laughed, watching as Craig Lerner pinched himself and grimaced.

Styles laughed. "All right—so it isn't a dream—like I said, only a suggestion. So what do we do—Tim—, you're the captain."

"You're the science officer, Jeff—you're supposed to advise me," Dodd told him.

Styles blinked, then shuffled through a ring binder. All the pages inside it were plastic coated; the binder fitted with a plastic zip lock track to seal it, but the track was open now. Styles flipped through the binder, stopping, going back several pages, then stopping again. "It says we should ascertain the status of other shuttles which were part of the fleet. We took off with all five of the others, didn't we?"

"Yeah—" Dodd cranked his chair away from Styles

11

and toward the control console. There was a toggle switch. He hit it, then threw a larger device which reminded him of a massive circuit breaker. There was a pneumatic humming sound.

Styles was talking. "Meteor showers, failure of solar batteries, an onboard computer malfunction — could have bee —"

The shutters over the double windshield parted, opened completely. Styles had ceased to talk and Dodd breathed loudly. Lerner said — "They all —" But he never finished.

There were five shuttles in a ragged wedge formation, stretched, he guessed, for perhaps fifty miles or more on both sides of them. There was a brightness to his right, but below he could see what he knew had to be Earth — Lerner had checked their position three times with the stars, with the onboard computers, with the navigational readout.

It was Earth — but it was no longer the blue ball it had been when seen from the moon — how many years ago? Had years ceased to have meaning? There were patches of green and larger patches of blue, but the shapes of the continents seemed subtly different.

"That's America — the United States," Lerner whispered from beside and behind him.

"But it's — Jesus — I can't see Florida — and — and the West Coast — it's — ahh —"

Dodd looked away from his home, and to the five ships. They seemed functional. He had to assume that aboard them now three crew members were awake, that aboard them now in each cargo bay twenty human lives lay in cold storage. He closed his eyes.

"Do you think there's anyone alive down there? I

12

mean — no cities — I don't get much infrared heat radiation at all. And the air seems thin off the instruments. Styles is gettin' something on the radio — but we can't make it out — the signal's too weak — could be a natural source — I don't know."

Dodd looked at him. Then he called to Jeff Styles, "Jeff — open the hailing frequency — we been awake for a couple hours —"

"Three hours and forty-nine minutes, captain. It's almost four A.M. eastern time down there."

"Open the hailing frequency to the other shuttles — let's get this show on the road."

"Right, Tim — you got it — live and on the air —"

Timothy Dodd picked up the handset — he liked that better than something that secured over his ears. "This is Eden One, hailing Eden Fleet. Eden One hailing Eden Fleet — come back if you read me, over."

There was static, then a woman's voice. "Tim — this is Jane Harwood — my first officer just got up — he's feeling nausea. I've been up for maybe three hours — I'm stiff as a broad — over."

"That's board, not broad, Eden Three — stay on the party line. And tell your first officer to eat some crackers — tell him about morning sickness. Anybody else out there awake? Come back."

"Eden Two rarin' to go, captain — took the liberty of awakening the landing party and starting the systems check on something called T.E.M. What the hell is that, over?"

"Remember Lunar Exploration Modules, Eden Two? Well, this is a Terran Exploration Module — it's in my orders. How the hell you think the landing party was gonna get down there?"

13

It was lousy radio procedure, he thought, laughing. "Well?"

"Yeah, well, captain—anyway, Dr. Halverson and Lieutenant Kurinami are all hot to trot—after they get over them anyway—"

"Over what?"

"The trots—couldn't let Eden Three get all the jokes—Eden Two out."

"You stay on the line too, and keep your exploration team rollin'. Eden One out—let's hear from somebody else out there—cóme back." There was more static, then another voice—and another bad joke.

The elapsed time indicator showed twelve hours had passed—things were on schedule, Dodd thought. Lerner sat beside him, ticking off items on a clipboard, Dodd watching him. "I activated the last of the systems, sir—a few diodes burned out, but they can be replaced—largely cosmetic. Some minor hull damage—meteor shower probably—I'll check the ship's log data banks later and scan for a record. But we still got all our tiles, though I don't know how well they'll hold up on reentry—no way of tellin'."

"If the landing party doesn't find out that things are habitable down there, we won't need any tiles anyway, will we?"

"You found them, huh?"

"The contingency plans for us? You betchya I did. I was lookin' through everthin' and finally I come up with contingency plan Alpha. There isn't any other one. If there's no way for us to come down, we just sit up here and go back to sleep after we put the whole fleet into geo-synchronous Earth orbit and shut down all the systems—dosage from the ampules will give us

14

another five hundred years. We can wake up and run a check on the atmosphere and if it isn't any good, we give ourselves the rest of the ampules and sleep for maybe another five hundred years. Trouble is, we only got one exploration module so when we ran out of the cryogenic serum, we'd have to try to land these things anyway. Now — I read the whole damn thing. Woulda been nice if they'd told us about this beforehand."

"You read the orders after lift-off."

"Now I know why they said not to read the rest of the orders — shit." Dodd looked away from the control console to Lerner, then past him to Styles. "Jeff — that lander about ready?"

"Kurinami and Halverson are already aboard running the last systems checks."

"Right." Dodd picked up his microphone. "Eden One to Eden Two — come back, Ralph."

"Right, captain — this is Eden Two — "

"Put your countdown onto the hailing frequency and launch T.E.M. when ready."

"We're making launch in twenty-five minutes unless there's a systems failure and we put a hold on — "

"Get back to me in ten, Ralph — Eden One out." Dodd set down his microphone and stared earthward. He exhaled so hard it made him shiver.

Chapter Two

Five minutes remained before launch. Ralph Jones had patched in the hailing frequency to the T.E.M. "Dr. Halverson—this is Tim Dodd—we never met. Over."

The voice surprised him. "Yes, captain—wishing us luck? Over?"

He shut off his mike, looking at Styles. "A woman?"

"Elaine Halverson—you want a list of her degrees?"

"What the hell is Kurinami?"

"A Japanese naval pilot—one of the best flight records you've ever seen—at least that's pretty much what his computer readout tells me—"

"Gimme that," Dodd snapped, taking it from Styles, Styles's marking pen sailing through the air, Lerner grabbing it for him.

"Are you still there, captain," Elaine Halverson's voice came back.

She was black—the personality profile said that. "Yes—ahh—yes, Dr. Halverson—I, ahh—wasn't expecting a woman, that's all—never had briefing on this, over."

"Maybe they thought a black woman would be symbolic, captain—maybe not. All I know is that before I joined the program they asked me if I could change my last name to something Latin sounding and embrace Judaism — but I guess they kept me anyway, over."

"Smart ass broad." He depressed his push-to-talk button. "What a fine sense of humor, Dr. Halverson — I admire your courage. You guessed correctly — I did call to wish you and your colleague Lieutenant Kurinami the best of luck — and our prayers go with you — Dodd on Eden One — out —"

He hit the switch for the overhead speaker so he wouldn't hear the countdown.

Part of the Earth could be seen in shadow — but there were no lights dotting its surface, as if man had never built his cities, constructed his power grids.

He hit the microphone again, patching in to the T.E.M. interrupting the countdown. Launch, by means of the arm which had been used to retrieve satellites almost since the beginning of the shuttle program, was to be in three minutes. "Dr. Halverson — this is Tim Dodd again — hey — I meant what I said — good luck to you and — what's his name."

"This is what's his name," a man's voice, Japanese accented but the English perfect, came back. "And thank you — T.E.M. out."

"Hope we'll be joining you down there — God bless you both. Eden One out."

He decided to listen to the rest of the countdown. He realized his own prejudices — but he closed his eyes to pray for them because if it proved impossible to land on Earth, they — the black woman and the Japanese pilot — would be doomed to die there, alone.

Chapter Three

"Dr. Halverson?"

The voice echoed through her helmet radio and she looked around, feeling awkward in the E.V.A. suit, still unsteady on her legs from the sleep and from the launch and subsequent reentry. She had flown a private aircraft and had a twin engine rating, but she considered herself no expert on rating other pilots. Yet, Akiro Kurinami just had to be, she thought, the best pilot who had ever lived.

"What is it, lieutenant?" She could hear her own voice echoing back to her—like she imagined it would be talking to oneself inside a fishbowl. Kurinami was climbing down from the ladder.

"Are you sure the coordinates were right, Dr. Halverson?"

"Call me Elaine—we may be the only two people on Earth, and if the atmosphere isn't breathable we're going to die right now. So we may as well be friends."

"My first name is Akiro, Elaine." She thought it seemed odd being in the space suit. He bowed.

"These are right coordinates—to answer your question. My sister and I grew up in Georgia—I recognize those mountains. And the radio signal came from somewhere near there—if it was really a signal at all. That tall one with the funny shape—it's Mt. Yonah."

"But I thought that Georgia was a very green

place — not desert."

"It seems to be desert toward the north and green toward the south — like some sort of natural boundary — maybe the green is encroaching on the desert." She didn't know. She was a climatologist among other things but she had no data. "Are the instruments sending?"

"Radiation levels — all of it — I checked them before I sealed the module, Elaine." He stood beside her now.

"The radiation levels don't seem abnormally high. And the oxygen seems that it should be breathable. I suggest something very unscientific, Akiro. If the earth is habitable, and the six shuttle craft are able to land, we will survive. If it is not, they will not and we won't — survive, I mean. I propose that since the instruments can do all that we can and relay all the information that we can, well — I suggest that we remove our helmets. And if we are still alive, get out of these space suits and explore."

"Agreed." He seemed to bow slightly, quickly again. "But I shall remove my helmet first — despite the fact that you command, you are a woman."

"We'll do it together." She nodded, bumping her head inside the helmet.

"At the count of three then."

"Yes — one — "

"Two — "

Simultaneously, they said, "Three," and she began to remove the helmet, watching as Kurinami did the same.

She shook her hair free of the helmet — she wanted to wash her hair, desperately. She inhaled — she coughed, the air chilled.

She was alive.

"We live—and how brave we were, Elaine—eighteen hours of oxygen in the suits and we would have died anyway." Kurinami laughed.

He had nice eyes, she thought—they showed laughter.

"How old are you?"

"Five hundred and twenty-four, Elaine." He laughed again.

"I am—"

"You are a woman—you do not need to tell me—"

"Five hundred and thirty-three." She laughed. "Give or take a couple of years." She set her helmet down. "Even though we've just been introduced, don't think me fresh if I start to undress—the space suit, I mean."

She watched his face—and then he began to laugh. They were both alive.

"An advantage of my race—wider nostrils—I can take in more air." She watched Kurinami as he panted, walking beside her. She ran her hands through her black curls—her hair wasn't dirty—it just felt dirty. She glanced at the Rolex Sea Dweller on her left wrist—it would be getting dark soon and the position of the sun confirmed that. A man's Rolex was too large a watch for a woman to wear, but each member of the Eden Project wore one and, according to the data she had skimmed before leaving the comparative safety of Eden Two, one of the personnel aboard had been sent to the Rolex repair school and had the complete tools and spare parts needed to service any watch, should it be needed. She walked on, a little cold without the space suit but able to move freely, feeling strength returning to her. Like Kurinami, she wore white coveralls over specially constructed underwear designed to aid the wearer in heat or cold. Over this, and she was grateful for it as she hugged it around her, a specially insulated arctic parka. The liner, which made the coat good until a temperature of seventy-five below, she carried in her backpack, not knowing what to expect of the night. There were insulated pants to wear over the coveralls if needed, and the stockings she wore inside her combat boots could be connected to the battery pack on her belt to warm her feet. She kept moving.

"Walking one hour," Kurinami began, interrupting her thoughts. "It seems like six hours."

"Yes—the thin air. But we'll get used to that. On old Earth, some peoples lived at altitudes and thrived where the average person would have been gasping for breath."

"This was more than a nuclear war—to do all of this. The cities are obliterated, it seemed—we saw nothing as we reentered. We should have seen Atlanta or Greenville, South Carolina, according to my maps."

"They are gone—but you are right—it was more than what anyone conceived a nuclear war would do. Or maybe it wasn't—maybe that's why we were sent."

Kurinami shrugged, saying nothing as he shifted the straps on his pack a little.

They had rested too long already, she thought—fifteen minutes. As she looked at her watch, she turned over her left hand and studied her lighter-skinned palm, trying to remember what her grandmother had told her about palmistry—was there a lifeline? She

21

couldn't find it but felt confident in her own ignorance of the subject — being unable to find it didn't mean it wasn't there.

She smiled as she tugged at her left ear — a habit she always had ever since she was a little girl when she had her ears pierced and lost the left earring. She had always found herself checking that the left one was still there. But her earrings were not there — she had not worn them and the holes had closed. But also, as she had suited up, she noticed the scar on the inside of her left wrist she got when she had put her hand out to catch a falling glass beaker and nearly bled to death as a result — the scar was gone.

It was curious.

"Why don't we climb that hill over behind us — if we can do it. And we can use the field glasses — see if anyone is alive. I doubt anyone is. If we move quickly, we can reach the lander by dark and use it for shelter against the night — there might be high winds."

"There might indeed," she answered. "That's a good idea. Captain Dodd will be expecting to hear from us anyway — so they can start mapping procedures to find a suitable landing zone. With California and Florida gone, both the landing strips are gone as well. So — let's go climb the hill." She stood up, feeling suddenly light-headed. But the feeling passed and she started after Kurinami, up the next hill.

"Gimme those, Akiro," she snapped, sounding harsher than she had intended. "I think I see something." She looked to the Japanese as he handed her the binoculars.

"Nothing can live —"

"I don't believe it —" And she adjusted the center fo-

22

cus again, carefully. Perhaps two hundred yards away, where sand and grass seemed to meet, there was an impression of some sort in the sand—it had caught the shadow as the sun set. "This is Christmas Day, did you know that?"

"You see Santa Claus?" Kurinami laughed.

But she didn't look at him, moving the glasses along the edge of sand and grass, along a rise. "Get your glasses out—take a look where I'm looking."

"Those are my glasses—I'll take yours," she heard him say, still not taking her eyes off what seemed to be tire treads, but unlike a car's. There was only one set visible, not a parallel set. "A motorcycle—"

"If that's a Japanese joke, I don't think it's so damn funny, Elaine."

"It's not a Japanese joke—look—where the grass begins out of the sand—"

"You're—"

"I know I'm right—but it's impossible—holy—"

"A man—" It was Kurinami, sounding more excited than she had heard him sound since they had left the lander.

She kept looking through the binoculars. There was a big black motorcycle on the ridge of a dune perhaps four hundred yards away—she adjusted her focus. Beside the motorcycle stood a man—a human being. She blinked, squeezing her eyes tight. He wore some kind of holster across his shoulders—it looked like he carried two guns, and there was a third gun on his hip and what looked like still another—yes, she thought—an assault rifle—hanging from his right side. Sunglasses masked his eyes, but he was smiling, a cigar clamped in the left side of his mouth, his teeth even and white, his hair dark brown, his face like something chiseled from rock—but a sculptor who was able to capture strength, intelligence.

Around his neck hung a pair of green binoculars—he had been looking back at them, she realized.

"He's saying something," Kurinami called excitedly from beside her. "I can see his lips moving. He must have seen us through those binoculars around his neck. Damnit—he's the first human being we've seen on Earth, and he's welcoming us and we don't know what he's saying!"

Elaine Halverson didn't move her binoculars. "My sister was deaf, from birth. She learned to sign and to read lips—she taught me how to do both."

The man wearing the sunglasses and smoking the cigar turned away, but she still watched him. He was mounting the motorcycle—it gleamed as if it had been freshly polished, catching the rays of the dying sun.

"If you can read lips, what the hell did he say, Elaine?"

"That son of a—"

"He said that? He said son of a—" Kurinami interrupted.

"No—he didn't say that—I said that." The man with the cigar and the sunglasses mounted the bike, looking back toward them once, shaking his head and then gesturing with his right arm toward a granite peak in the distance.

"He's signaling to us. What the heck did he say, Elaine? Tell me."

The man on the bike started off toward the setting sun which was bright yellow and dominated the horizon so that she had to squint as she watched him.

"Bastard," she murmured.

"What'd he say when he saw us?"

She watched the man on the machine vanish into the horizon. She told Kurinami, "What he said was, 'There goes the neighborhood.' That's what he said, the son of a bitch!"

Chapter Four

It was almost dark — snowflakes slowly falling — but there was enough light to see and walk. Kurinami had insisted they follow the man on the motorcycle, leave a marker and take compass bearings and then return to the lander in the dark if they could not intercept the man. She had agreed.

And she heard something now — it was the sound of an engine, loud, and then another sound identical to it.

There was movement over the horizon. "Look out, Elaine!" Kurinami pushed her down, shoving his M-16 forward. She reached to the hip holster at her side for the pistol — she had never fired a gun in her life except during the brief training session. "You never know what deep space exploration might cause you to encounter." And afterward in the yearly familiarization sessions.

But she had the pistol in her right hand, trying to get the slide back with her left.

She could see clearly now as she looked up — two motorcycles. It was nearly too dark to see at all, and the single headlights of the motorcycles glared so brightly she could see nothing past them except in blurred silhouette.

"We are armed!" Kurinami shouted.

There was a voice — somehow she knew it belonged to

the man with the sunglasses and the cigar. It was low, slightly arrogant sounding to her, but the arrogance was confidence, she knew. It was touched with humor. "We're the welcome wagon—and that M-16 is decidedly unfriendly looking—though I wouldn't walk around here at night unarmed myself."

The man moved in front of the light from his motorcycle and the engine noise was completely gone now as she watched him, backlit, his assault rifle profiled, every curve of his body profiled. He was tall—well over six feet. Lean—it was the man she saw earlier, she knew. He was long legged. He was armed with more than just the rifle.

"My friend and I," he went on. "We came out here to meet you folks. Say hello, Natalia."

"Hello."

"You from the Eden Project?"

"How did you—" Elaine Halverson began.

But the soft-spoken man with the icy edge to his voice interrupted her. "Merry Christmas, by the way. My daughter cut down a pine tree and got my wife to help her make decorations. And my son Michael made them take a turkey out of the freezer. Michael makes his own corn liquor but we've got plenty of Seagrams Seven left. My son's girl makes a dressing that smells out of this world—no pun intended. And Paul Rubenstein showed my daughter Annie how make improvised field expedient matzo balls so we've got all the trimmings. And Natalia, here—and I didn't even know she could cook. She's a wonderful person. She made sweet potato pie."

And the man turned to face Kurinami who had put down his rifle. "And how about you fella—would you like a good cigar?"

Chapter Five

"Unless you think it's really important," John Rourke said, leaning against the kitchen counter and sipping at a double shot of Seagrams Seven over ice with a splash, "we can go back to the lander after dinner—the turkey's almost ready, they tell me."

He watched the black woman's eyes—and he laughed. "You're having a hard time with all of this—"

She walked toward the counter, picking up the drink he had made her—the Japanese man, Akiro Kurinami, had gone off with Paul and Michael to inspect the hydroelectric system. Natalia and Annie and Sarah and Madison formed an icy quartet behind him.

Elaine Halverson sipped at her drink. "I keep expecting to see Rod Sterling come out and—"

"Relax," Rourke interjected.

"But—" She gestured around the room. "All these weapons, and a television and a stereo—and a turkey and—electricity—"

"If you like after dinner, I can check the tape library and maybe we can find your favorite movie—I have over a thousand hours of video recordings—I know." Rourke walked past her and across the Great Room toward the stereo. "Music—music is just the thing."

"Are you trying to make me think you're crazy?"

"No—not at all—I've never really felt comfortable playing the host—and now suddenly I have two guests and one hundred and thirty-six more on the way—ahh—perfect." He drew the record from its dust jacket and placed it on the machine carefully, working the switch to move the tonearm into position. "Antonio Carlos Joabim." Rourke smiled. "There's nothing quite like a samba to relax you." He picked up his drink and sipped at it again, walking to the sofa and sitting down on the side nearest the gun cabinet.

"You were untouched by the war, then—I mean, there was a war, right?"

John Rourke took a larger swallow of his drink. "Oh, yes—there was a war indeed. And one of the post-holocaust scenarios—a worst case scenario—came to pass. The ionization of the atmosphere, the air catching on fire, destroying all life on the planet."

"But then—oh, my God—you aren't—"

"What—a talking dead man? Hardly. But it's a long story—a very long story. I'm as alive as you are. We can explain after dinner, after contacting the Eden Project ships. After coming out of The Sleep, I'd imagine you and the lieutenant aren't terribly tired. And neither am I, actually—so let's leave it until then—"

"Daddy—dinner's going onto the counter—"

"Thanks, sweetheart," Rourke called to his daughter. Then he looked at Elaine Halverson, saying, "I'm afraid I never did get a dining room table up here—but informal dining was something I always preferred. I'll get Lieutenant Kurinami and the others—excuse me a moment."

Rourke started across the Great Room, past the kitchen, and as he turned into the work room to start after Michael, Paul Rubenstein, and Lieutenant

Kurinami, he could hear Elaine Halverson's voice behind him. "Is there anything I can do to help—I was always pretty good around the kitchen." John Rourke started to laugh.

Chapter Six

"That's right — I just had Christmas dinner — turkey — it was delicious — over."

John Rourke watched the woman as she spoke — aside from the fascination with another human being from his own time, there was something more. She had bounced back from what he had fully realized at the time to be a startling experience, and she had bounced back from it with humor. She was a pretty woman, younger than himself perhaps. Her skin was a dark chocolate and her cheekbones high, and he imagined that before the five-hundred-year sleep her hair — a gleaming coal black and tightly curled — had been substantially shorter because she seemed uncomfortable with it now, running her hands through it constantly.

"The radio must really be crazy, Dr. Halverson — it sounded to me like you said turkey and Christmas dinner again."

"I did — over."

"Explain, Dr. Halverson — is Kurinami with you?"

"He's fine — he stayed at the Retreat of Dr. Rourke and his family and their friends." She cleared her throat. "Dr. Rourke and his family survived the nuclear war and the destruction of the planet — he indicates that a worst case post-holocaust scenario came about, the total ionization of the atmosphere, and the subsequent burning away of the atmosphere during one twenty-four hour period. Except for one member of his Retreat group—a young girl of about twenty—"

"She's nineteen," Rourke corrected.

"I've just been corrected—she's nineteen—except for her, the entire group survived because they had access to cryogenic chambers like our own and the cryogenic serum. The young woman—and I'm not quite clear on it yet—she survived with some sort of Retreat group that lived underground for five centuries—she should be twenty-fifth generation, a descendant from the Earth population of five centuries ago. Dr. Rourke—he's an M.D.—he told me that he sees no observable differences in the girl despite five centuries of close interbreeding from a core population of one hundred persons. Dr. Rourke brought me here on his motorcycle. After our transmission, I'll be returning with him to the Retreat. He indicated he could remove the radio unit from the lander and connect it to his system at the Retreat and in that way we could be in constant radio contact. Over."

There was static again. "It seems like this doctor has been around—ask him if knows of any potential landing sites in his area. Over."

"Here," Elaine Halverson said, handing Rourke the microphone. "You talk to him."

"What's his name again—Captain Dodd?"

"Right—Timothy Dodd."

Rourke settled the microphone in his right hand. "Captain Dodd—this is John Rourke—Dr. Halverson thought we should talk. Over."

"Dodd here, doctor—if you already have some sort of base in the area and since our two primary landing sites are gone, I'm left with an alternative. Attempt a landing in Spain — and God knows what we'd find or where we'd be — or attempt a landing somewhere else in the United States. The desert southwest immediately presents itself, but landing in sand isn't something any of us would relish. The best bet in view of your base and its location and the evident habitability would seem to be finding a landing site as near to you as feasible. Do you concur and do you have any suggestions — Dodd over."

Rourke worked the striking wheel of the Zippo, snow falling on his eyelashes and on the back of his hands as he stood just outside the lander and its ladder base, the microphone transferred to his left fist. Elaine Halverson sat with her legs hanging down the ladder, her body half in the shelter of the open lander hatch. Rourke inhaled on the cigar, pressing the push-to-talk button, exhaling as he did. "Some of the interstate highway system is still intact. And there won't be any power lines to worry over. I have no heavy equipment for actual runway building. Possibly the main runway at the airport in Atlanta might be suitable, but I doubt it, and the background radiation level may still be too high. Most of the city was vaporized." Rourke realized he was thinking out loud. "Isotopes which might have formed during the missiles' strikes could be anyone's guess — some theories advanced before the Night of The War — it sort of came to be called that — but before the Night of The War there was conjecture that some isotopes might have a radioactive half-life of five hundred thousand years or better. But I do have a more concrete suggestion. Rourke over."

There was static, then Dodd's voice. "Which is, doctor—over."

Rourke exhaled a cloud of the greyish smoke from the cigar, watching it dissipate on the air, the snow falling thicker now. It was still Christmas and it would be for two more hours or so. "I was aware that both your primary landing zones had been eradicated so I prepared some data. There's a stretch of Interstate Highway Sixteen in Bulloch County—Interstate Sixteen connects Macon to Savannah. Macon is pretty well gone, but Savannah was intact from the bombing at least—and this stretch isn't near either city really. The stretch is ten miles long, almost perfectly straight and would give you an actual landing surface thirty-eight feet wide with a wingspan clearance of over one hundred feet. That ten-mile stretch has two bridges that pass over the highway. These would have to be blown and cleared. South of here the desert seems to have taken over so there shouldn't be much worry over trees when you're coming in. I can reach the area in a few hours and make a detailed inspection of the road surface. Any tar would have burned off during the holocaust, but the concrete surface should have remained. The interstate itself bridged a creek and that bridge could have weakened. If any of the road surface is drifted over with sand, I have a snow plow attachment for my truck, I can use that move the sand. With Dr. Halverson knowing the technical aspects of what you need, acting as a liaison, so to speak, and Kurinami to help my son, my friend Paul, and myself, plus the four ladies in our group, we should have sufficient manpower. Over."

There was a long pause while there was nothing but static, then Dodd's voice. "You realize, doctor, that

34

once de-orbiting is begun the situation for us is irretrievable. Over."

"Affirmative, Captain Dodd. If you've got a better solution or can come up with one, I'll certainly help all that I can. If you ventured beyond the Mississippi then you'd have the problem of getting your people and equipment through the radiation zone along the route of the Mississippi River—there was the heaviest bombing there and the area should be hot for thousands of years to come. If you stay on the other side of the Mississippi, you'll be faced with rougher climatological conditions than you would here, reduced growing seasons, etc. We still have two growing seasons here. Plus as I understand it from Dr. Halverson, the primary buried supply dumps are located in the East, so you'd be closer to your source of supply. Landing in West Texas might prove ideal for the actual landing, but afterward might prove unwise. I can't make your decision, but I will aid you as best as possible. If you do land beyond the Mississippi, unless I can somehow locate and repair or assemble from scratch some sort of aircraft, none of us will be able to join you there to offer assistance from the ground—the no-man's land along the course of the Mississippi can't be crossed except by air without highly specialized transportation which just isn't available. Over."

"Doctor—the way we're orbiting now we can survey a good ninety percent of the global surface, all the fleet combined. We'll continue the survey and get some pictures of that stretch of highway if you can give us precise coordinates. We'll talk again late tomorrow. Over."

Rourke reached into the musette bag that hung at

his left side, extracting a small leather-bound note-book, flipping through it by the light of his Zippo, stopping when he found the appropriate page. "If you have commercial atlas references in your computer system, the stretch of highway is bounded by U.S. Highway Three-Oh-One to the west and State Highway Sixty-seven to the east. Longitude and latitude are as follows: for Highway Sixty-seven—thirty-two degrees, fifteen minutes, twenty-three seconds north and eighty-one degrees, forty-two minutes, forty-five seconds west. For U.S. Three-Oh-One coordinates as follows: thirty-two degrees, eighteen minutes, twenty-eight seconds north and eighty-one degrees, fifty-two minutes and twenty-eight seconds west. I assume you are voice recording, or do you require I repeat? That's as precise as I have them." He looked at Elaine Halverson—she was staring at him for some reason. "I'll give you back to Dr. Halverson, captain—Rourke over." And Rourke returned the microphone to the woman, walking away from the lander as he heard her conversation with Dodd resume. There would be time with Dodd the following evening to inquire if in his mapping procedures Dodd encountered evidence of any other life on the planet.

Rourke looked skyward—the stars were obscured by the snow clouds. But he wondered if life existed somewhere else. And he realized with momentary sadness that he would never know. With the shuttle fleet landing, there would be no hope in his lifetime at least of ever getting man into space again. No factories to recondition the shuttles, to fabricate external fuel tanks or solid rocket boosters, no way to build a space station or platform from which deep space craft could eventually be built.

Locked to the earth, as if manacled, Rourke thought. He studied the tip of his cigar—it glowed orange in the darkness. But the Earth itself was new—and regardless of what Dodd's mapping indicated, it would have secrets, secrets he could learn. Elaine Halverson had mentioned underground storage sites where supplies, prefabricated shelters, vehicles, and equipment—where all of these had been stored before the Night of The War. She had learned of these after her awakening during perusal of the mission materials. Aircraft and aircraft parts were included there. He could borrow one of these, or borrow parts at least and then build an aircraft of his own.

John Rourke closed his eyes. In a few weeks time he could administer a pregnancy test to Madison—she had said she felt somehow different. He smiled at the thought. He was too young to be a grandfather, but perhaps soon he would. He would stay until the baby was born, teaching Michael more about medicine. And there were doctors comprising part of the Eden Project. After the baby, then he could begin.

Sarah talked of loss. He felt loss as well. In sacrificing his daughter's childhood, he had not only lost a part of her, but lost something else. His best friend—perhaps the only true friend he had had throughout his life, Rourke reflected—his best friend, Paul, would marry Annie. That much seemed clear. And they would stay together and have children. But he—Rourke—would pay the price in the loss of Paul to explore the new Earth beside him, to fight beside him.

Sarah—she had not kissed him upon their return to the Retreat, she had not smiled. Throughout dinner with Halverson and Kurinami, she had spoken little, not at all to him.

Her anger had not cooled, her heart had not warmed.

Natalia — Rourke opened his eyes, snow falling more heavily now.

First to bring the Eden Project down safely. Then to investigate Michael's findings of the parachute and find the wreckage of the plane.* Perhaps it could be made to fly again — at the very least it would yield clues as to the pilot's origin.

"I'm ready, Dr. Rourke."

Rourke turned to the sound of Elaine Halverson's voice. "Fine — we'd better get started then on that radio." Rourke threw down the stump of his cigar and started toward the lander — he judged it would take under forty-five minutes to disconnect the radio and pack the needed parts that would amplify his signal aboard the Harley. He would still be home before Christmas ended.

*Survivalist #10: The Awakening

Chapter Seven

He could trace his lineage to well before the Era of Destruction, trace it to the early and glorious days of the 1930s and 1940s, trace it to what had been called the War To End All Wars — he smiled at the thought — and back farther than that. He was thankful — to no one in particular except the accident of Fate — that he had been born after it had been possible to function again in the outside world. To have been shut up in the Complex as his forebears had been for more than twenty generations, to do nothing but study, prepare, work toward the distant eventuality of the return to glory would have been unbearable to him, he knew.

The jungle had returned, just as he had seen it in the photographs and the videotapes — and ever since childhood when his parents had taken him from the Complex into the outside world, it was the jungle that he loved, loved almost as much as The Purpose.

"Helmut — what is it that you are thinking? Your body is here with me, but your mind seems so far away."

He looked at her. "I was merely thinking how much it is that I enjoy the jungle. Its loveliness now is unsurpassed except by the loveliness of your face, your body — but before it was all destroyed — how lovely must it have been then?"

She smiled, her green eyes lit with what he knew was

love for him, and she leaned her head against his shoulder, her blond hair sweet scented like the jungle flowers. He held her close in silence, staring beyond the clearing and the bench on which they sat, staring at the world that surrounded them. It was what had been meant in the apocryphal stories in the Judeo-Christian mythology—a Garden of Eden.

After a time, Helene moved her head from his shoulder, sitting, her hands folded in her lap, but saying nothing. He stood, feeling her watching him now as he straightened his khaki uniform blouse, then adjusted his pistol belt. "I sometimes—" She ceased to talk in mid-sentence. Helmut Sturm turned to look at her. He wondered suddenly what less perfect human females actually looked like, if indeed any of them had survived. How was it to see a woman whose skin was not fair, whose eyes were dark, whose body did not reflect the values of religiously adhered to athleticism since childhood. "I sometimes," Helene, his wife, began again, "wish—sometimes—I sometimes wish that it were not our historic destiny to—" But she let the sentence hang again.

Helmut Sturm reached out to her, her eyes lowered, not looking at him. With his fingertips he raised her chin and could now see her eyes. "Helene—The Purpose is what we have always lived for, planned for—dreamed of. And now—how fortunate we are, that after twenty-five generations, it is our generation which is charged with fulfilling our destiny. That the child you carry in your womb shall indeed inherit the Earth." He watched as her eyes left his, and he followed them as her gaze settled to her swollen abdomen, swollen with life.

"But I fear for you, and my brother Sigfried and for all of you. What dangers may lie in store. We have no way to know. The two pilots who were lost—they—"

Helmut Sturm touched his right index finger to her lips, to silence her gently. "Darling." He dropped to his knees before her. "For five centuries, our people have existed for The Purpose. They have sacrificed, they have studied, they have prepared. After so much sacrifice for so long, how can we—whom fate has chosen—give less than our all? For five centuries we have developed superior science, superior technology, superior weaponry. We are ready to oversweep the world."

And on his knees still, he held both her hands in his, turning to face the one ornament that was not a part of nature, the one embellishment to the garden in the jungle near the main entrance to the Complex which was their home. And he felt a thrill of pride, of his racial destiny—as he stared at the bronze bust on the single bronze column rising twenty feet into the blue sky. The carriage, the nobility, he thought—to have lived then, to have known The Führer as had his ancestors.

Chapter Eight

Vladmir Karamatsov stepped down from the Arctic Cat, the crunch of gravel and shale beneath his feet here at the base of the mountain—odd seeming after the years of nothing but snow. It was warmer here at this lower altitude and the air quality—the atmosphere richer—invigorated him as he strode from the Cat toward the assemblage of Land Rovers some one hundred yards away. He had told the driver of the Arctic Cat to stop at a distance from the Land Rovers so the men and women standing beside the machines could see him as he approached, see that he moved with full strength, that his stride and his carriage were strong.

He opened his parka and reached under it to adjust the strap of his shoulder holster, the Smith & Wesson 59 there. The backup gun—a Model 36 Chiefs—was polking at his right side near the scar from the removal of his kidney and it irritated him. But the ones by the Land Rover knew of the lost kidney, lost as a result of the gunfight five centuries earlier with the American John Rourke, the American who if he still lived would have his wife, Natalia Anastasia Tiemerovna, living with him.

So Vladmir Karamatsov did not adjust the butt of the blued steel .38 Special, so none of those watching him would misinterpret the gesture as reaction to the operation, as weakness.

He stopped, ten yards still from the Land Rovers, not even out of breath.

Yuri Vanyovitch, young, brash, assistant to the party secretary, stepped forward. Vanyovitch stopped less than a foot before Karamatsov extending both hands to Karamatsov's upper arms, leaning forward, kissing him on each cheek, then stepping back extending his right hand. Karamatsov took it.

"Assistant Secretary Vanyovitch—it is good to see you as young seeming as ever after these four years."

"Comrade Colonel Karamatsov—the mountains have done for you what you claimed—your health, your vigor—our hopes have been fulfilled."

Karamatsov let himself smile. "So now it is time for *my* hopes to be fulfilled." And Karamatsov, without waiting, began walking toward the Land Rovers, Vanyovitch gesturing toward the most gleamingly clean of them. Karamatsov adjusted the angle of his stride to intercept the Land Rover as if he had known all along which one it would be that would chauffeur him to the main entrance of the underground complex in the Urals that had been his unconscious home for five centuries; his home and the home of the few survivors of his KGB Elite Corps who had protected him, found for him the best medical care after John Rourke had nearly killed him. It was this complex where the Soviet cryogenic chambers had been taken after their theft from the supplies designated for the Womb, here where the precious vial of cryogenic serum he himself had acquired when first learning of the Eden Project in the years before the Night of The War had been used—to preserve him and those few of his Elite

Corps for awakening.

He boarded the Land Rover, Vanyovitch sliding in beside him, the chauffeur closing the rear door and running to slip behind the wheel. He closed his eyes, but only for an instant, lest it be thought he still endured some hidden weakness. The Land Rover started into motion, and Karamatsov turned to Vanyovitch. "And how go things, comrade, at the underground city?"

"Well — preparations are all but complete for your expeditionary force to be under way." And Vanyovitch looked away.

Karamatsov smiled. While he had slept, others had not. During the late 1950s, Soviet leadership had decided that global thermonuclear warfare was inevitable. Plans were begun at once to disperse war-related industry to reduce targeting effectiveness. Plans were also begun to survive this inevitability. By 1963 the underground city was begun, completed after the near miss of the Cuban Missile Crisis with greater urgency, the final work accomplished by the winter of 1968. By the spring of 1969, it was occupied. Utilizing natural geologic formations beneath the mountains which formed the Ural chain, the caverns had been artificially formed into a complex of inter-connected vaults; a city inside granite, powered by geothermal forces and plutonium generators, a city of thousands of ordinary Soviet citizens, from the political to the industrial, from all walks of life. It had been used as a testing ground for environmental concerns, as a testing ground for new growth techniques for plants — all preparatory to the then thought to be eventual Soviet occupation of near Earth space in massive artificial satellites or space stations. By 1976, the year of the two hundredth anniversary of the United States — Karamatsov smiled at that — the underground city had been completely independent of the world above the ground. Children were born who had never ventured into the outside world yet were healthy, strong, physically fit.

And then the Night of The War — but the underground city had gone on.

To withdraw to the underground city had always been an option, but the Womb had seemed so much more attractive — to sleep through the confinement beneath the surface and then go forth as the master of Earth.

But it had not been possible.

Once his own death had been presumed and it had been learned that the architect of his death was Gen. Ishmael Varakov, Rozhdestvenskiy was sent to fill the void his presumed death had made, but the seizure of power to control the Womb had been beyond the grasp. There were endless series of operations, the moments when pain had so consumed him that only hate had kept him alive.

By the time his strength had even begun to return to him, the holocaust had come. The underground city was his only hope, and he had used it. A population of more than five thousand were loyal if unskilled, obedient if untrained. He had spent five years after the fires had consumed the Earth, five years of pain from his wounds, teaching others to teach the successive generations the ways of war. And then he had slept.

He had awakened to a population of seven thousand, healthy, well fed, a world within a world — food

45

in plenty, farm and domestic animals preserved—even meat from cattle grown underground, the leavings of the animals converted to fertilizer for the underground fields and gardens. A controlled environment with its own water cycle, some of the cavern ceilings so high that wisps of clouds from condensed vapor would form.

A world. And he awoke to find himself as its hero, its archetype and, if not officially, its master.

The Womb, he was convinced, had ceased to exist. All attempts at contacting it after the holocaust had been unsuccessful. All attempts since his awakening—he had forbidden that it be attempted in the intervening years lest he be murdered in his sleep—had been unsuccessful as well.

High level reconnaissance flights sent out in the four years since his awakening had shown no evidence of life in North America of any kind. Life had been found in Europe—the French had planned with underground shelters, but they had not been elaborate enough to withstand and their occupants had been reduced to barbarism, leaving the shelters when the air had become again marginally breathable, living off the scant plant life. Some resorted to cannibalism. It was from these that he had drawn his "women"—for these semi-humans had spread across Europe in small tribes. But there had seemed to be nothing like this in North America.

But the mountains of Northeastern Georgia had not been burned away in the holocaust, and somewhere inside them he felt it—that John Rourke, that Natalia—that they still lived, had survived as he had survived. The old general—Varakov—would have seen to that.

Preserve the bitch Varakov called a niece—and preserve her lover.

He called to the chauffeur.

The Land Rover stopped.

Karamatsov did not wait for the chauffeur, walking from the Land Rover to stare along the valley floor toward the entrance to the underground city. The entrance would not have been distinguishable from the air. The tanks which had been built, the aircraft which had been built—they were housed inside. Along with his expeditionary force of one thousand men whose equipment had had five centuries of development to surpass what had existed before, whose training had been five centuries in the making. He would at last conquer. He smiled—but first things first. Vanyovitch's presence—he felt it beside him.

"A question, comrade colonel?"

He looked at Vanyovitch, not quite trusting him but liking him. "Yes?"

"I am not a student of weaponry—but I am given to understand by your military staff that the weapons which we now possess are unlike anything seen in the history of the old Earth."

"This is true, comrade."

"Then why—I could not help but notice, comrade, when you reached under your coat as you left the Arctic Cat—why—"

"Why do I wear a twentieth century firearm? Why do I not instead carry one of the new assault rifles? Why not something more technologically sophisticated?"

"Yes."

Karamatsov smiled, not looking at Vanyovitch, but

47

looking along the greeness of the valley and toward the entrance instead. "There is a man—I have mentioned him."

"The American John Rourke—but surely—"

"Rourke would have survived—despite my hatred for him, he was like no other man. And he—John Rourke—he will be carrying weapons of the twentieth century, weapons which in his hands nearly caused my death. And when I find him, I shall meet him on even terms. I shall best him at his own game," and he drew the Smith & Wesson autoloader—it had been stolen from a shipment of commercial firearms bound for West Germany years before the Night of The War. He drew the pistol slowly. "I shall destroy him on his own terms—and then I shall never need this pistol again. It is as simple as that, comrade. For one shining moment I carry this."

Chapter Nine

Sarah Rourke stomped on the emergency brake of the camouflage-painted Ford pickup, Annie and Madison seated on the front seat beside her, Madison riding near the window. It was the first time Madison had ever ridden in a truck, ridden anything besides the motorcycle which she had ridden behind Michael after her rescue from the savagery Michael had spoken of. Madison almost reverentially elaborated on Michael's heroism and John Rourke's heroism.

John Rourke—Sarah Rourke watched him through the pickup's windshield as he dismounted his jet black Harley-Davison motorcycle, bristling with weaponry as he usually did. Natalia already dismounted, she, too, bristling with weaponry.

The other two bikes still carried their riders—Paul and Michael.

"All right, girls—time to get out," Sarah announced, reaching up onto the dashboard lip for the blue and white bandanna handkerchief she had taken from her hair—it had been giving her a headache.

She climbed down, rubbing her palms along her blue-jeaned thighs, stretching, tired, even though splitting the driving with Annie, from the nine hours of driving over destroyed roadways, along creekbeds, bypassing what had once been cities. But they had reached what had been Interstate Highway 16. She would tell John to teach Madison how to drive an automobile—the truck. She somehow assumed that Michael could.

Annie climbed down, Sarah looking at her disgustedly—a mid-calf-length blue floral print-flounced skirt, one of her off-white peasant blouses, and a shawl. Her daughter looked like she were going to a picnic rather than to move drifted sand from a roadway and blow up bridges.

Madison had climbed down on the other side, Sarah walking to the front of the pickup, looking at her de-facto "daughter-in-law"—she was Michael's common-law wife now. Although a skinny girl, long legged and long armed, there was a certain prettiness about her—and despite the situation, Sarah felt instinctively that she liked the girl. Madison's major failing was that she called her—Sarah—"Mother Rourke." Madison was dressed similarly to Annie—the clothes were Annie's. At least some of them—a mid-calf-length skirt of heavy grey material with a pink pin stripe running through it. But over the peasant-style blouse she wore a man's grey crew neck sweater. The sweater's origin was complex—it was John's sweater. Sarah had bought it for him. Michael used it. Now Madison wore it, the neck miles too big for her, the length making it go to her hips, the sleeves pushed up past the elbows.

"Mother Rourke," Madison began.

Sarah looked at her, noticing from the edge of her peripheral vision as Kurinami and Elaine Halverson climbed out of the back of the pickup. She—Sarah—had offered Elaine Halverson a spot in the truck cab, but Halverson had preferred to be less cramped. Sarah shrugged it off as she thought about it. She said to Madison, "You can call me Sarah, or even call me Mother if you want—or Momma, like Annie and Michael do. But not Mother Rourke—it makes me feel like a cloistered nun in her eighties."

Madison smiled, apparently considering Sarah's words, Sarah beginning to tie the blue and white bandanna in place over her hair. Her hair was now longer than she had worn it since a girl, but she had no intention of cutting it for some time to come. As she knotted the bandanna at the nape of her neck, Madison spoke. "I would like to be your friend."

"Fine—you can be my friend, Madison."

"But you are angry at me."

"No—I'm not. I'm angry at Michael's father—I'm not angry at you. And I'm getting angry at Michael—Michael's just like his father."

"Yes—he certainly seems be be, Mrs. Rourke."

Sarah snapped her head left—Lieutenant Kurinami was standing beside her. Past him she could see Elaine Halverson walking toward John, Michael, Paul, and—Natalia.

"I imagine though that you are quite proud of your son—a fine, strapping man, broad shouldered, a keeness in his eyes. He would make a fine pilot, I think. I understand that both your husband and young Michael are involved with the martial arts—for five centuries, I have had no one to spar with. Do you think that your husband might consider sparring with me tonight after camp is established?"

She looked at Kurinami and felt herself smile. "I can't speak for Michael—but I'm sure my husband wouldn't mind—he spars with me all the time." She started away from the truck, thinking, Let's get this foolishness on the road.

Chapter Ten

Michael had drawn a circle in the sand with his knife. The sun declining now, the sky purple to the west, a wind whipping across the barren flatness of southern Georgia, John Rourke stood, his shirt off, his weapons left with the shirt beyond the edge of the circle, his boots there as well. Barefoot, Rourke watched Kurinami step into the circle.

"Would that we had available to us gloves, doctor — then we could have a real match."

Rourke almost whispered, "We can have a good practice bout without them — just exercise a little caution."

"You will think me unmodest —"

"Immodest," Rourke corrected automatically.

"Yes — but I was fleet champion for two years — before coming to the United States for your astronaut training."

"I'll be very careful." Rourke nodded, watching the Japanese lieutenant as he approached. "What style do you prefer?"

"It is largely my own style, but to be sure it is based in the traditional arts — Gung Fu."

"Mostly Tae Kwon Doe." Rourke nodded. "This should prove interesting."

"We shall begin then —"

Suddenly Natalia was standing up, entering the circle, handing off her pistol belt with the twin L frames to Madison. "Here — hold these, darling." She stepped between them. "One can't have a sporting contest without a referee."

Kurinami stepped back. "But a woman —"

Rourke felt a smile cross his lips. "Be lucky I'm taking you on — and not her. She'll be a fine referee." Suddenly he caught sight of Sarah's eyes — she was watching him and he smiled at her but she didn't return the smile but only stared.

Rourke looked back to Kurinami. "Whenever you're ready, lieutenant."

Natalia stepped back, to the edge of the circle.

Kurinami shifted to his own right, turning half left, his bare feet in a close T-stance, his head cocking left slightly, then right, his right arm extending, the right hand rising slowly, the fingers moving, like things with a will of their own. Then both hands moved, the left hand rising sharply, the right hand lowering, then the reverse, the fingers of the right hand doing their dance again, Kurinami edging slightly forward.

Kurinami's right wrist flicked, the hand striking forward, like the head of a snake, Rourke's left instinctively going up to block as he sidestepped slightly right. Kurinami's left hacked toward him in a swinging arc, Rourke's right rising, catching the blow on the inside of his right wrist, rolling it off, his right fist striking forward as he did. Kurinami's body wheeled half right, the left foot suddenly there, the leg at full extension, a roundhouse kick, Kurinami wheeling as Rourke deflected the kick with his left forearm. Rourke backstepped, Kurinami's right leg up now, the left slightly flexed, Kurinami's right foot slapping toward him.

Rourke wheeled half right, catching Kurinami's right foot at the ankle in his cupped left hand, throwing the Japanese naval lieutenant off balance, Kurinami spinning, falling to his right knee, his left foot snapping up and out, Rourke catching the blow in the abdomen, falling back.

Kurinami was up, the hands moving again, the upward and downward slaps through the air, the sounds like the hiss of a slow-moving whip, the left hand hooking outward. Rourke pulled his face back, feeling the rush of air, dropping to his right knee, a leg sweep with his left as Kurinami's right foot extended for a kick. Rourke's left leg impacted the back of Kurinami's left knee, Rourke rolling right, onto his left elbow, Kurinami toppling. Rourke pushed himself up, his left arm extended, his left knee the fulcrum, his right leg flashing up and out, catching Kurinami in the abdomen, a double kick. Rourke's leg drew back, a third kick into the chest, Kurinami's body already jackknifing but snapping back now. Kurinami's body was straight as a rod. The Japanese naval aviator fell backward, impacting the ground hard.

Rourke was up, dropping to his left knee against Kurinami's chest. Rourke's left hand cocked the head back at the chin, his right fist hammering down. He stopped the fist an inch from Kurinami's windpipe. His voice barely a whisper, John Rourke said with a smile, "What do you say we call it a draw, Akiro?"

The Japanese coughed once, then started to sit up as Rourke stood to his full height. Kurinami began laughing uncontrollably.

Chapter Eleven

Hampsturm Führer Helmut Sturm could see his wife Helene's face in the crowd beyond the platform erected for the band, the platform to which soon the leader would ascend, the brass section laboring the strains of "Deutschland Über Alles," this their anthem despite the betrayal by post World War II Germany of the Nazi ideal. His right arm extended, his obersturm führer shouting for the salute, the leader ascended the platform, the strains of the anthem rising somehow, the gas fires from the massive concrete torches flanking the entrance to The Complex rising, licking the jungle air. The pace of the brass slowed but rose to a crescendo, cymbals clashing.

Then a voice from the podium, the voice of the leader. "Sieg!"

As one, Sturm's company and the other companies flanking his, and the men, women, and children gathered beyond the perimeter of the parade ground answered, "Heil!"

"Sieg!" Again the call.

"Heil!"

"Sieg!"

"Heil!"

Cheers, applause. The leader raised his hands toward them, palms outward, the cry coming from in the crowd now — a woman's voice. Perhaps it was Helene, he thought with pride. "Sieg!"

"Heil!" The shout echoed along the parade ground, from beyond, from the bandstand as well now, the leader turning to murmur something to one of his aides.

"Sieg!" Again it came—a chorus.

"Heil!" The answering chorus.

The leader extended his hands, palms outward, his head raised, his chin cocked back—reminiscent, Sturm thought, reminiscent of the Führer who was their martyred spirit.

"We leave here today to march forward into history as victors!"

Again the cry from the spectators. "Sieg!"

"Heil!"

The nod of a head, a smile, the leader's voice reverberating over the public address system. "It began in the darkest hour—when our leader, our glorious Führer, five centuries ago was betrayed and murdered and thus disallowed to fulfill his historic mission, to snatch the Reich from the ashes and lead his people once again to victory." There was a hush.

Sturm could see Helene's brother, Sigfried, at the far end of parade ground, his platoon forming the honor guard before the podium, the set of Sigfried's face, the pride which glowed from it.

"But out of this dark hour, phoenixlike, rose the New Reich!"

"Sieg!" The cry again.

"Heil!" The unanimous answer.

The leader's hands again extended palm outward and there was silence. The wind was rising, the black and red and white of the flag stiff now on the wind.

"The underground movement was formed to build again, to plan. And the jealous adversaries of our glorious Führer rose to snap like the mongrel dogs they were at each other's throats. And finally the cut to the jugular. The thermonuclear war which destroyed all of humanity—which would never have taken place under the leadership of our glorious Führer who sought order for the world above all personal gain or glory. But when the war came between the so-called super powers, we had already begun to plan to rebuild the earth. From this place, The Complex," the leader said and gestured broadly toward the main entrance between the two concrete and brass gas-fired torches, "the seed for new life shall come. For four centuries, we confined ourselves from the light of the sun, preparing for the new order, the children and grandchildren and great-grandchildren of our glorious Führer's closest confidants adapting to the hardships, surmounting the obstacles, building a perfect internal environment immune from the ravages of the near airless world which surrounded us. Our science and our technology moved forward, the classic genius of our race triumphing over all adversity. And then the Great Return to The Light. A century to allow our numbers to grow to unprecedented levels—" Sturm thought of the life which grew inside his wife, of the four children they already had, their oldest Manfred already twelve and an assistant to his underleader in The Youth. How beautiful the boy looked in his uniform. How proudly he wore the armband.

"And now," the leader continued, his voice almost hushed, "the fruits of our science, of our technology—of our historic struggle—the fruits are borne!" He ges-

58

tured skyward and Helmut Sturm caught his breath in this throat. Crossing over the treetops came the Condor Squadron, its soundless turbo jet helicopters crossing to the airspace above the parade ground, hovering, the wind of their rotor blades whipping at the banner which flowed behind the leader, the flames of the torches flickering more brightly. "We go forth to defeat whatever enemies might exist, whoever might dare oppose us. To plant the seed of National Socialism throughout all lands, that the world may finally know the perfect order of our leadership. Sieg!"

"Heil!"

Again the leader called, "Sieg!"

Helmut Sturm's throat ached with the word as he screamed it into the wind — "Heil!"

Chapter Twelve

Natalia Anastasia Tiemerovna put her hands on her waist, resting them over the flaps of her holsters there, looking squarely at John Rourke. "It cannot be done—not the way you want it done with the explosives we have."

She looked from his eyes back toward the campsite a mile distant down the sand-covered highway. "If there's one type of explosive I know, it's our variant of C-4. When you and Paul took it from that patrol after the Night of The War, you didn't take enough. And in five centuries, it could have begun breaking down chemically anyway."

She watched Rourke's eyebrows raise above the frames of his dark-lensed glasses. "Paul and I took all they had. It was an engineering outfit—we assumed they were planning to blow up some bridge or another. Bumped right into them—no choice but to fight it out. There were eight of them. We cleaned out all the explosives they had and I stored them in the Retreat with this purpose in mind."

"But the engineering patrol didn't have enough to start with, John. I've blown up bridges and so have you. With what we have here, considering the construction of the bridges crossing the highway, all we have enough to do is make a mess. Not all—but vaporize the bridges which is what you want. These bridges have steel girders supporting the reinforced concrete. At twenty-eight feet wide, do you realize the mass of concrete and steel that represents? I mean, certainly, just a little could weaken the bridge structurally so that it couldn't be used. What we have could blow out the center of the bridge, or blow out one side of the bridge and drop the bridge across the highway. But you want to turn the bridge into dust. Because otherwise, you'll have tons of concrete and steel impacting the road surface, and you'll destroy the surface sufficiently that it can't be used. And if the bridge doesn't come down completely, there's always the chance of a wing tip snagging on a still standing pylon and the shuttle would crash. What you are asking is impossible with what we have. I have the skills to vaporize the bridge cleanly, but I don't have the equipment. We'll have to think of another way." She looked away from him, studying the bridge, wishing she had a cigarette, but after five centuries of not smoking, she would not start again even if cigarettes had been available. And she had left the cartons of cigarettes John Rourke had acquired for her at the Retreat.

"Let's go for a walk," John Rourke almost whispered, taking her right hand in his left. She looked up at him, smiled, letting him hold her hand. He was starting across the bridge, the vista on both sides one of desert, drifting dunes crisscrossing the faint impression of the highway boundaries. "We can clear the sand with the plow on the truck. It'll take some time, but we can do it."

"Agreed — but to what purpose if we cannot destroy the bridges?"

"We'll find a way of doing that. I may head out with

Paul or Michael to Colorado, to the Womb—"

"No—and besides—you could never cross the no man's land along the Mississippi."

"I've given that some thought—Elaine Halverson says that from the Eden Project abstracts she read, some of the underground storage units contained fully assembled prop planes and even small helicopters. But the trouble with that is we don't have the equipment to dig out the entrances to the storage areas. And our own explosives might produce the opposite effect from what we want. There could even be industrial explosives stored down there, although she didn't recall reading there were any. But if she weren't looking for explosives on the list, then she might not have noticed them anyway. But I can confirm that with Captain Dodd tonight on the radio. Don't mind me, I'm thinking out loud." She felt the pressure as his hand squeezed hers.

"Maybe I can utilize our explosives to gain entry to one of the underground storage areas. And what we can't blow away we can clear away with the snow plow attachment for the truck," she told him.

"So if Dodd can confirm there are industrial explosives stored there—"

"Then I can use them to clear away the bridges and you won't need an aircraft."

"And if there aren't explosives—"

"Then both of us," she said. "Both of us will go to the Womb and search for more plastique or for industrial explosives."

"I don't want—"

"To have me with you?"

"Not—not that. You know that. But that place—"

62

"I am not a Communist now. I am not in the KGB any longer. It holds no special meaning for me — not if you are with me." She leaned up to him. John Rourke took her in his arms, and she felt his mouth crush down against hers and she closed her eyes.

Chapter Thirteen

Vladmir Karamatsov sat at the head of the confer-ence table—to his right the party secretary, Boris Korenikov; to his left, Yuri Vanyovitch.

Karamatsov spoke. "The expeditionary force will be split into two elements as we have already planned. The cargo aircraft will land on the desert regions of West Texas, an area with which I have great familiar-ity. After landing, our helicopters will be dispatched under the direction of my second in command Major Antonovitch to the site of the Womb. The Womb will be penetrated and any useful material will be ac-quired. What cannot be used but might prove useful to any enemy should one exist will be destroyed if the Womb cannot be made useable. The scientific party will endeavor to activate the particle beam weapons which were to have been used to destroy the Eden Proj-ect upon its return. If they can be made to function, they will be used for their original purpose. If they cannot, Major Antonovitch will notify me of this and I will postpone my mission in Northeastern Georgia, and with the remainder of our air corps and additional helicopter units, destroy the Eden Project as it lands. Although North America seems all but devoid of life, unfortunately South America does not. High altitude flights have indicated industrial activity of high tech-nological level in Argentina. The origin of this activity is unknown to us, but may prove useful. After securing North America and destroying the Eden Project, what remains of the Womb or some similar suitable location shall be made our Western Hemisphere base of operations and an expeditionary force shall be launched against whatever society exists in Argentina. Meanwhile, a third element of our force shall sweep Europe, locating those remaining units of the wild tribes and subjugating them. They could prove useful as slave labor if sufficient intelligence remains to them. If this proves impossible, they can be liquidated at some later convenient opportunity. For certain activities of my own, I may have need of some of these members of the wild tribes. Much depends on the outcome of my activities in Northeastern Georgia. High altitude observation flights using radar misdirection systems to evade detection by the Eden Project have in fact confirmed that all six of the craft are in Earth orbit. One craft is in geo-synchronous Earth orbit roughly over the northern third of Georgia. This would confirm my earlier hypothesis that my old enemy still lives, has survived in much the same manner as have I and those few members of my original KGB Elite Corps."

Karamatsov stood. "I am prepared that Major Antonovitch and myself leave at once, Major Krakovski to assume command of the third Expeditionary Element to subjugate the wild tribes. Questions?"

"Could not, comrade," Yuri Vanyovitch began slowly, "the craft which comprise the Eden Project fleet be used to our advantage if somehow the fleet were allowed to land and then its occupants only destroyed?"

65

Karamatsov looked at him, smiling. "A surface analysis of the situation might indeed infer that, comrade. Yet, no risk can be taken that might somehow allow any of these one hundred thirty-eight persons to escape us. All were hand picked from among the allies of the United States prior to the Night of The War for their physical perfection, mental abilities, and skills. Were even some small number of these to survive, the potential for future risk from this group would be high. Doubtless, there were provided underground caches of equipment for use upon their return, as my intelligence prior to the Night of The War indicated. The contents of these caches are unknown to us. Perhaps nerve gas, perhaps biological agents which could be used to destroy us. The risk of this outweighs any potential advantages the contents of the six shuttle craft or the craft themselves might afford us. No — they must be destroyed before they reach the ground. This is imperative."

The party secretary stood. "You have our confidence, comrade — and our loyalty."

Karamatsov nodded only — for he already knew that.

Chapter Fourteen

John Rourke depressed the push-to-talk button on the radio set's hand microphone. "Would you repeat your last transmission, captain — over."

He released the button. After a moment of static crackle, the voice of the Eden Project commander came back. "Contents of supply caches in your vicinity do not indicate industrial explosives. Nearest supply cache containing such items near Boulder, Colorado — over."

Rourke set down the microphone, not speaking into it, silent, watching the faces of Sarah, Paul, Michael, Annie, Madison, Dr. Halverson, and Lieutenant Kurinami. And then he looked at Natalia. "It'll have to be the Womb — there's no other way." She closed her eyes, the firelight somehow less bright now with their surreal blueness shielded. He picked up the microphone. "Rourke to Eden One — we have an alternate plan for obtaining the proper explosives. It should consume several days. How long until your orbits begin to deteriorate — over?"

"Dodd to ground. Estimate decay point will be reached in one hundred twenty-three hours, plus or minus as much as sixty minutes — over."

Rourke nodded — uselessly — toward the microphone. "Rourke to Dodd — all right. We'll hit the nearest supply cache by midday tomorrow. Barring the unforseen we should be able to penetrate it within twenty-four hours by working in shifts. Placing one of the aircraft there into flightworthy condition should consume another eight hours. That consumes roughly forty-four hours. From your description of the available aircraft, I estimate four hours' travel to Colorado. Another hour at least to reach the designated area. Forty-nine hours. Twenty-four hours added on to locate the needed materials, another hour of return time and four hours travel back to this site. Add another hour for the unexpected and seventy-eight hours are consumed. While Major Tiemerovna and I are gone, the others of our party will be at work clearing the sand from the road surface. That leaves well over two days for successfully destroying the bridge and removing any miscellaneous debris that may result and for you to land. Opinion — over."

"Checks for a more suitable landing site from the air have proven negative. I repeat — negative. In the event your operation is not successful, we will be forced to land in Utah. The landing site there is doubtful but the best which presents itself from aerial observation. The landing site in Spain is unuseable as best as can be ascertained — repeat, unuseable. Your landing area is our best shot — over."

Rourke studied the microphone in his hands, then depressed the push-to-talk button. "We won't let you down — Rourke over." He handed off the microphone to Elaine Halverson. Natalia had opened her eyes — and he saw a resignation in her eyes that chilled him.

Chapter Fifteen

Opening of the supply cache had netted more than Rourke had bargained for, but less than he had hoped for. The manifest Shuttle Fleet Commander Dodd had checked had proven accurate regarding the absence of explosives, but inaccurate in that an earth mover — not in particularly fine shape but apparently still service-able — had been left inside the underground cache.

Natalia had used half of the explosives supply min-ing the area near the entrance. Then, with the truck, Paul Rubenstein driving it, the excess dirt and debris and rocks had been cleared back, utilizing the snow plow attachment.

Rourke, Paul Rubenstein, and Michael Rourke stood now inside the underground warehouse, the light from Rourke's Kel-Lite all that illuminated the area.

He swept the light from the earth mover and toward the gasoline-powered generators. "While Natalia and I are gone, Paul — you and Michael get one of these generators set up. With the truck and this earth mover, the two of you guys and the women and Kurinami, too — you can work in shifts and electric lights should come in handy." Rourke moved the light toward one of the pickup trucks at the far end of the cache area. "We'll get one of those trucks working and while the earth mover is being moved back to the landing site, one of you can hit the nearest strategic fuel dump and get the gasoline you'll need to keep the equipment rolling." He swept the light toward the airplane on the far side of the underground vault. "Likely, the engines have been specially modified not to need aviation grade fuel. If they have, that'll take Natalia and me some time. Either way, we'll take all the fuel we can carry out of here so we can fly ourselves back with the explosives. Just leave enough to get the earth mover and our pickup truck back to the landing site and to get one of these pickups to the fuel dump."

"So long as one of us stays behind with Kurinami and the women, they'll be protected enough, Dad — you should take Paul or take me along with Natalia — we're talking excess manpower here and maybe not enough there, and neither one of us weighs so much we'll adversely effect the aircraft's fuel economy or cargo capacity on the way back. What if you land in some hostile area — people maybe like the ones Madison and her people were so afraid of. A third person could make the difference — even if it just means someone left to guard the airplane while you and Natalia penetrate the Womb."

Rourke looked at his son, hearing Paul's voice. "He sounds just like you — and he's right just like you. Only one of us needs to stay here — the other one should go with you and Natalia. And I'm the one who should go."

Rourke looked away from Michael, then to Paul, then back to Michael. He put his right hand on his son's shoulder. "Madison already asked me if I could determine if she were pregnant after we got the Eden Project down safely. I told her I could. She missed her

70

period—but that could be emotionally based or for any number of other reasons. I think you were right—a third hand along could make the difference between success and failure—but it'll be Paul. Madison's consumed with uncertainty now—she needs you here. And taking you away from your mother now won't win me any points, either. You'll be in charge—your mother, Kurinami, and your sister can split the shifts with you. Dr. Halverson can be utility backup and spell people. Since Madison doesn't know how to drive, she can't be much help there, but she can keep the food going, the generator fueled and Dr. Halverson can help out there as well. You've gotta teach her how to drive—wait on the motorcycles until we find out for sure if she's pregnant. But she's got the abilities—in your off hours teach her how to handle a truck."

And Rourke looked away, taking the light and handing it to Paul. "Get going on that truck—I'll get some additional lighting down here so we can start working on the airplane."

It would be the three of them—himself, Natalia, and Paul. It seemed that it had always been that way.

Darkness surrounded him, but John Rourke knew where he was going as he left the supply cache.

Chapter Sixteen

Nicolai Antonovitch stared at the message his subordinate had given him. He remembered to look up, to dismiss the man. He looked back at the message, realizing his hands were shaking. The names meant much to him. Antonovitch realized too that he was holding his breath, for he could hear more clearly now the subtle vibration of the aircraft which cocooned him.

Comrade Colonel Karamatsov was in the bathroom — how could he — Antonovitch — tell him?

The names — the man who had forestalled the dreams that he — Antonovitch — had shared with his commander. And the woman, once his — Antonovitch's — commander.

John Thomas Rourke. Natalia Anastasia Tiemerovna.

Antonovitch heard the door of the bathroom opening, closing.

He looked up. "Report, comrade colonel, from one of our high altitude observation aircraft. An intercepted transmission between a ground base and the single element of the Eden Project Fleet in geo-synchronous orbit. The names, comrade colonel — "

He watched Vladmir Karamatsov as Karamatsov sat down opposite him, the aircraft vibration the only noise there was. But then there was another noise, the sound of steel rubbed against leather. Karamatsov was drawing his pistol from the shoulder holster under his left arm. "You know, Nicolai—this very same pistol was the one five centuries ago which I was unable to fire quite fast enough. And John Rourke nearly killed me. It was clear to me as I lay there until help arrived, that he had assumed me to be dead. I had felt him close my eyes. The doctors later ascribed my condition to being like some sort of seizure—I was very near death. When he closed my eyes—it was the shock, I suppose—but when he closed my eyes, a most peculiar occurrence took place. Have you ever read of the research that was undertaken prior to the Night of The War concerning near-death experiences?"

Nicolai Antonovitch began to speak, that, yes, he was familiar with this supposed phenomenon, but Karamatsov merely began to speak again and Antonovitch said not a word. "They always seemed somehow celestial, these experiences, that somehow these very ordinary people who had clinically died and then were revived were about to enter some Judeo-Christian Heaven. But my experience was not like this. There was a dark tunnel and at its end rather than some heavenly white light, there was only more darkness, and it seemed not to have an end. And there were no comforting visages of my mother or my father or of any friends who had died. There were snarling sounds, like the sounds of mad dogs, and there were shrieks of pain and anguish." And Karamatsov laughed. "Once, when I impersonated an American, I was forced to attend a religious service—necessity, of course. They sang a song—I even joined them. One of the lines was to the effect, Who is on the Lord's side? I discovered, in my near-death experience, that I served a different lord if indeed there is one at all."

Nicolai Antonovitch said nothing—and he knew nothing to say.

Chapter Seventeen

John Rourke checked the air speed indicator—the Beechcraft Baron 58 was holding a hair over one hundred ninety-five miles per hour, and he checked that the twin prop plane's cowl flaps were closed. Adjusting his flaps, the shadow of the Baron grew larger over the terrain racing beneath them, Natalia's voice beside him coming to him as he peered through the pilot's side storm window. "What are we looking for, John?"

"That aircraft Michael spotted, right?"

It was Paul Rubenstein then, and Rourke, glancing to the controls, then peering back to the ground below, answered both of them. "It is the plane Michael spotted. I gave the coordinates from Michael's map to Eden One and they reconned it—about five miles north of where Michael spotted the parachute, Eden One spotted wreckage—we should cross over it any second now." He exhaled loudly, the controls easy feeling in his hands as he leveled off, throttling down near stall speed. "And I also used the cassette player in the truck to play the tape of that radio transmission Michael got, jerry-rigged it to the radio so that Eden One could record it and run it through their onboard computers. It was just what I'd thought," Rourke continued, banking slightly to port, following a defile of rocky tree splotched ground beneath them. "It was a code—they haven't broken it yet and I doubt they will.

But the base language for the code seemed readily apparent."

"What was it?" Natalia whispered.

Rourke looked away from the ground beneath the aircraft and into Natalia's eyes. In her hands she held his binoculars, and her hands trembled slightly. "Russian," he told her, then looked away.

Behind him, over the hum of the engines, he could hear Paul Rubenstein murmuring, "Oh, shit."

Rourke continued to study the ground, banking again to turn another twenty degrees or so to port, catching something in the sunlight down in the cleft of the defile, throttling down so close to stall speed the engines were coughing, sputtering. He adjusted the mixture, the engines settling, skimming the ground now as close as he dared.

He could see it clearly now. What caused the reflection was a stray shard of glass, perhaps from the windshield. The aircraft was a seemingly upgraded version of the Soviet MIG-25, and from the design changes, he assumed used for high altitude, high speed reconnaissance.

As quickly as the shadow of the Beechcraft crossed over the wreckage, the wreckage vanished behind them.

"That was very similar to a Foxbat-B," Natalia said from the copilot's seat to his right. "But it looked as though the design had been extensively modified. For observation flights at high altitude, perhaps."

Rourke started to say something, but Paul Rubenstein began, "A Soviet spy plane—from where? The Womb?"

Rourke didn't answer the question—for the time being at least he had no answer. But reaching the Womb in approximately five hours might help.

He gave the Beechcraft Baron full throttle, the RPM reading hovering near twenty-five hundred, adjusting his mixture as the aircraft began to climb toward cruising altitude. In five hours, John Rourke reflected, he might know a great deal.

Chapter Eighteen

The CAR-15 slung cross body from his left shoulder under his right arm, his right fist closed over the pistol grip as he stopped. They had approached from a different angle than the approach five centuries ago. From the height of the rocks above Rourke could at last see the extent of the damage inflicted when Reed had successfully caused the destruction of the Particle Beam weapons system and blown away the top of the mountain which had been the Soviet KGB Elite Corps Womb, and before that, before the Night of The War, NORAD Headquarters, Cheyenne Mountain, Colorado.

The entire top of the mountain was a huge crater now, filled with the rain of decades, perhaps centuries, like a volcanic lake.

Rourke stood now where the road leading to the main entrance had once been. It had been five centuries before when, with Natalia, who was not terribly well disguised as a Soviet soldier, they had bluffed their way into the Womb: Rourke, Natalia, a last group of American volunteers from the forces of U.S. II, and a group of courageous Soviet Special Forces personnel dispatched by Natalia's uncle, Gen. Ishmael Varakov.

Rourke stared at the topless mountain.

"What a place," the younger man, flanking him on the left, murmured.

John Rourke looked at Paul Rubenstein. "You should

have seen it then, Paul."

And Natalia began to speak, as if reciting a litany, Rourke thought. "There were barbed wire fences there, and there, and over there, and a mine field going completely around the complex, there. And sentries and guard dogs. And inside—inside, there was fighting, fighting like I had never thought there could be. And many brave men—they all died. And Rozhdestvenskiy—he followed us from here and then John—I was asleep by then, Paul, and so were you—John fought him. He told Annie about it when she was little still and Annie told me. John stood at the top of the mountain and shot down the last KGB helicopter—"

Rourke interrupted her. "Apparently I didn't do a good enough job—that aircraft. It was Soviet."

"Vladmir—toward the end he would tell me nothing, and I realized he had never truly confided in me."

Rourke looked at her, the sadness that filled her eyes. Natalia Anastasia Tiemerovna continued to speak. "That others of the human race have survived—it makes my heart want to sing—but if it was the KGB—I—"

Rourke's right arm moved across her shoulders and he folded her against him. "We have a job to do here—now—we can worry over what's in store for us later. Let's move out."

The main entrance seemed still sealed, but perhaps the one by the airfield—what had been the airfield—would have lost its integrity. To penetrate the Womb otherwise might prove impossible—John Rourke started ahead.

Chapter Nineteen

One of the dreams, the second time he had taken the sleep, had looked like this—helicopter gunships filling the skies. Unlike the dream, the gunships were not something from the twentieth century but vastly more modern, nearly totally silent as they swept over the airfield from the southeast. Rourke pushed Natalia back into the shelter of some vast chunks of rock, pieces of the blown-apart mountaintop.

"My God—"

Rourke looked at Natalia. "That's getting to be a habit with you."

"John—it must be—"

"Soviet—"

"There were civil defense projects, some very elaborate ones, but I knew nothing specific concerning them—Vladmir never told—"

"Maybe he never knew," Rourke rasped, tucking back more into the scant overhead shelter the rocks provided.

"But whoever would come here would have to—"

Rourke worked the bolt of the CAR-15, chambering a round off the top of the thirty-round stick, then setting the safety on. "Could have come here because of some of those observation flights—could be a lot of reasons. Could have had access to KGB records—stay down." Rourke shoved her back still more, Paul Rubenstein well behind them, but Rourke was unable to see the younger man, assuming Rubenstein to have taken cover as well.

More than two dozen helicopters hovered now over the remains of the Womb airfield, one of the choppers from the center starting to descend rapidly. Rourke offed the CAR-15's safety. He could feel Natalia's hands on his back — her hands felt to him as if they trembled.

Ghosts, Rourke thought, malevolent ghosts from five centuries past.

The all black helicopters, their red Soviet stars gleaming like blood, opened their formation as the helicopter which had begun to land touched down.

Before the runners touched, armed men in black fatigue uniforms and black baseball-style caps jumped from the craft, fanning out in an almost perfect circle, hitting the ground in prone positions, assault rifles snapping up to their shoulders. The rifles — Rourke stared at these, the rifles themselves bearing definite lines of origin from the Kalashnikov, but somehow smaller and lighter.

"They look like KGB Elite Corps," Natalia whispered from behind him. "But that can't be — they are all — "

"Yeah." Rourke nodded, not knowing what to say.

A man stepped down from the helicopter, trim, athletic seeming, gold braid decorating the baseball cap's peak, and some type of rank insignia on his collar tabs, but the rank something from the distance Rourke could not make out.

He felt Natalia's hands tense against his back, felt the rush of breath against the side of his neck, heard her gasp, "That is Nicolai Antonovitch — he was Vladmir's liason officer in the Kremlin — but he should have — "

Rourke felt her head rest against him. He finished the sentence for her, "Died."

Chapter Twenty

It had taken seemingly forever to leave the place in which they had hidden and move back toward Paul Rubenstein's position, Rubenstein's Schmeisser at the ready. But Rourke wanted no gunfight. They had moved on again, slowly, as the airborne Soviet armada had one or two silenced gunships at a time touched down. More of the black-clad Soviet personnel swarmed over the pockmarked remnants of the airfield. Natalia, as Rourke had moved beside her, seemed shaken, Rubenstein at once angry and — logically, Rourke concluded — frightened.

The Soviet force was likely the most powerful military unit on the face of the Earth, perhaps the only military unit on the face of the Earth.

Rourke, Natalia, and Paul Rubenstein reached the rocks beyond the airfield, taking a circuitous route to avoid detection from either ground or air, Rourke easing now into a niche in the rocks, checking the cylinder of the Metalifed and Mag-Na-Ported Colt Python, reholstering the .357 in the flap rig on his belt. Methodically — Natalia beginning to talk, but distracted sounding, nervous sounding — Rourke checked in turn each of the twin stainless Detonics Combat Masters, taking the pistols one at a time from the double Alessi shoulder rig which rode across his shoulders under his battered brown leather bomber jacket. "That they could be here — it's impossible — it's — "

"But they're here," Paul Rubenstein snapped, cutting her off.

Rourke reholstered the last of the twin stainless Detonics .45s, leaving the pistol hammer down. He looked at Paul, then at Natalia. "They are here, and the time for determining just how they were able to accomplish that isn't now. We came here for the explosives — and regardless of this Soviet presence, the Eden Project Shuttles will have to de-orbit just the same. Without the explosives, they can't. If they are forced to land in Utah, they'll fly right over the Womb, and those gunships can shoot them down as they land. And maybe our newfound companions have some way of reactivating the Particle Beam weapons — but I doubt that. I haven't seen any heavy equipment or cargo choppers and without replacement coils, without huge generators, without a power source — it'd be impossible. But they might have Particle Beam weaponry located somewhere else on the planet. This obviously isn't their base — not the way they landed ready for possible battle. The Womb is dead."

"How are we gonna get those explosives without them knowing about us?"

Rourke looked at Rubenstein and let himself smile. "Wouldn't you say Natalia is an excellent pilot?"

"Of course — and so are you."

"I wasn't fishing for compliments, but I was hoping you'd say that. Those gunships should be faster than our aircraft, and they also have defensive and offensive capabilities our aircraft doesn't have. What if we steal two of them and use their onboard weapons systems to destroy the bridges before the Eden Project lands, then use the aircraft to provide covering fire in the event of attack?"

"You mean," Natalia said slowly, "take over two of the new helicopters while they are on the ground, then quickly assess the weapons systems and—"

"Better than that—we take over about a half dozen of them—render them inoperable," Rourke told her. "That shouldn't be too hard, since the more sophisticated something is the easier it is to ball up when necessary. Then we get airborne—couldn't have more than five or six of the craft still operable to pursue, and we destroy those as they take off. But we load the weapons systems gear out of the choppers we leave behind and that way have backup missiles and other weapons-related necessities to use with our two gunships."

"How the hell are we gonna do that, John?"

Rourke looked at Paul Rubenstein. "There are enough of those Soviet troopers on the ground—Natalia and I both speak Russian. Some of the Soviet troopers appeared to be women. Natalia and I each steal uniforms, and you back us up from cover in case anything goes wrong. It worked once before here. We gather up all the weapons and gear we can as we sabotage as many of their ships as possible, then we hit the skies."

"Oh, boy," Paul Rubenstein remarked.

Chapter Twenty-One

She felt a sickness in her stomach, like the feelings she only rarely had when she was about to have her period — but her period wasn't due yet — it had begun almost immediately after the awakening and been the heaviest flow she had ever had, but it had stopped after only a few days. The sick feeling in her stomach was not from that, she knew.

If Antonovitch were alive, then perhaps some of the others were alive as well. Who? How many? How? Where? Where had they survived, and by what means?

She watched John Rourke as he moved now, along the edge of the field, watched him. He had needed a victim of good height so the uniform would be a satisfactory fit.

She had already picked her victim, a tall, blond-haired woman less than thirty yards from her.

As if the KGB assault troops had willingly wished to cooperate, they had left scant security surrounding the airfield, the bulk of the personnel scaling the mountain apparently in search of a way inside. Some of them, Antonovitch among them, were near the airfield entrance to the underground portion of the complex. Occasionally there was the sound of a jackhammer, run off a portable generator which had been towed beneath one of the helicopters, punctuating the all but soundless landscape.

It was cold—but that was not why she shivered, Natalia Anastasia Tiemerovna realized.

John Rourke was up now, to his full height, her eyes transfixed she knew as she watched him.

John Rourke was running, a long-strided sprint, his gloved hands bare, extended ahead of him. The Soviet trooper started to turn toward him—her heart leapt to her mouth. She smiled at the thought—such was a physical impossibility. Rourke's left hand reached the trooper's right shoulder as he turned. Rourke's right fist crossed the man's jaw as the Russian's black-gloved hands twisted the assault rifle into a firing position. John Rourke's right knee smashed upward at the precise second his right fist crossed the KGB assault trooper's jaw. The trooper's head snapped back, his body jacknifing forward. The knife edge of John Rourke's right hand backhanded across the right side of the trooper's neck over the carotid artery.

The trooper's body began to sag. Rourke's long right leg again snapped up; another knee smash, to the left side of the trooper's head this time. The body collapsed.

Suddenly, for some reason she never understood but in response to something which had never failed her, she glanced toward her own intended victim. The woman was swinging her body toward John and the downed Soviet trooper. The woman's weight was on her left boot heel, her assault rifle starting to rise.

Natalia's right hand reached to the hip pocket of her black jumpsuit, the Pacific Cutlery Bali-Song coming into her fingers. Her thumb worked off the lock, her arm starting the arc. The Bali-Song was closed still, and she had heard somewhere once that before the Night of The War there had been perhaps five people in the entire United States who could throw a Philippine Butterfly Knife with the handle slabs closed so that it would open in midair to impale the target.

She was not one of the five — but she had never been counted either.

The Pacific Cutlery Bali-Song left her right hand, a glint of steel reflecting in the cold sun. There was a subtle clicking sound; the handle halves were a blur as they opened, something she could see almost in slow motion as the KGB woman's assault rifle rose into position.

The woman's body shuddered, the head snapping away. What looked like a bar of glinting steel — the skeletonized handle halves half open against the flesh — along the side of the neck just below the left ear, the assault rifle clattered to the pockmarked concrete. The KGB woman's body spun, sagged. Natalia was up, running, to catch the body. The body dropped, Natalia beside it the same instant, twisting the Wee-Hawk blade of the Bali-Song in the wound to seal the wound and reduce blood flow to avoid damaging the uniform.

Natalia glanced across the airfield once — John Rourke was looking at her as he hefted the silenced and presumably dead guard to his right shoulder.

The knife blade still buried to the handle halves in the KGB woman's neck, Natalia boosted the woman up, Natalia's left hand grabbing the dead woman by the right wrist, the body across Natalia's shoulders now.

Natalia gauged the dead woman's weight at somewhere around one hundred twenty pounds — despite it, despite the sick feeling of trepidation in her abdomen, Natalia ran, almost not feeling the added weight.

Chapter Twenty-Two

The one Natalia had identified would recognize Natalia—Major Antonovitch, she had called him. Rourke glanced at Natalia once—her longer than shoulder-length hair was caught up under the black baseball-like cap, but the uniform didn't at all disguise her figure: the longness of her legs, the slenderness of her waist, the subtle fullness of her hips; her stride confident in her borrowed black combat boots as she strode across the field.

Rourke looked away from her, looking instead in the direction in which he walked, toward another of the silenced black helicopters.

Slung under his right arm was the new Soviet assault rifle—it was approximately thirty caliber, the ammunition self-contained, the cartridge case nonexistent, the propellent solidified to form the case. Caseless ammo had been experimented with before the Night of The War by Heckler and Koch and others. This looked very derivitive, Rourke thought clinically. The magazine was forty-round capacity, again as best he could judge with the limited time, and the magazines were a synthetic and didn't appear reloadable. He assumed they were disposable.

He hoped the guns worked.

Under the black fatigue blouse, the twin Detonics stainless pistols were concealed, tucked beneath the waistband of the fatigue trousers in the event the space age Soviet assault rifle didn't work.

John Rourke kept walking, the baseball cap pulled low over his dark-lensed aviator sunglassed eyes, the nearest of the helicopters—a guard, presumably the pilot standing beside it—less than fifty yards away.

The pilot was smoking a cigarette. Rourke deduced this was not someone who had taken the sleep, but perhaps someone who had been spawned from five centuries of survival in some hermetic shelter. Even Natalia had not resumed cigarette smoking.

Rourke walked on, the pilot turning to face him. The man had no assault rifle but a full flap military holster on a belt at his right side. Rourke carried one just like it, a vastly updated version of the pre-war Stechkin: stainless steel, the caliber a variant of 9mm, slightly more powerful than the 9mmX19, 9mm Parabellum or Luger round, the pistol equipped with a three-way selector—safe, semi-automatic, and full. Rourke assumed full auto amounted to the three-round burst firing. The magazine, eighteen rounds, was too low in capacity to trust to the average man's abilities to sustain two and three-round bursts—it would be burned out in one trigger pull otherwise.

But Rourke trusted its deadliness—he could afford nothing else as the pilot's hand drifted toward the holstered Stechkin.

Up his right cuff, John Rourke carried the Black Chrome Sting IA, blade downward, the blade pressured against the inside of his wrist—cocking his right hand outward would drop the blade into his palm.

Of necessity, he planned silent work.

He moved ahead, the distance narrowed to twenty

yards, the pilot's right hand no nearer to the Stechkin in the flap holster, but no farther either.

Rourke flashed the man a smile. Rourke under-ranked him significantly. The pilot was a captain, Rourke's rank showed corporal.

"What is it, corporal?"

In Russian, Rourke answered, "Something very important, comrade captain—of life and death." The distance was ten yards now.

"What is it you say, corporal?" The man started to open the flap of his holster. "I do not know your face."

In Russian, Rourke told him, "You won't have much time to learn it." Rourke moved his right wrist outward, the Sting IA Black Chrome easing into his palm, Rourke's right arm snapping out, the black-chromed stainless steel double-edged boot knife sailing outward from beneath Rourke's palm. The Russian pilot's hands clasped to his chest. Rourke took three quick steps and was beside the man, easing the body down, looking behind him—had anyone seen? But no one had.

Rourke could see Natalia, at the far side of the airfield, standing awkwardly beside a man one and a half times her own considerable height—Rourke smiled. The man would have the Bali-Song somewhere vital and deadly.

Rourke eased the pilot's body up, flopping it back into the side door in the helicopter's fuselage. Rourke followed the body inside, staring ahead as, mechanically, he slit the KGB man's throat.

Rourke moved across the body, wiping the blade clean of blood on the dead man's clothes. He went forward to the cockpit—all the controls seemed digital, and there were fewer of them. There were television monitor panels set overhead and into the control panels—attitudinal, status, consumption; all the controls gauges had handled in aircraft of five centuries ago. The British had experimented with such control systems for commercial aircraft prior to the Night of The War.

Rourke licked his lips.

He nodded—it could be flown. He would fly it.

Weapons systems—air to ground missiles, air to air missiles. Rotating machine guns were mounted to the forward and aft sections of the fuselage. Controls for the guns were within easy reach of the pilot—it was a one-man craft if necessary.

Rourke took the butt of his assault rifle and hammered it against the central panel, knocking out the video screens for the air speed, altimeter, and heading functions. Dropping into a crouch, he felt beneath the control panel—wires. He ripped them free from both the source and the panel itself so they couldn't easily be bridged.

He started from the machine, but stopped—crates, secured against the interior panels of the fuselage—missiles of both the air to air and air to ground type. A smile crossed his lips—John Rourke could feel it.

Rourke jumped clear of the fuselage—he would be back. There had been a handcart used to haul up the jackhammer and its accessories—if he could steal that. But his smile broadened. Pushing the handcart across the pockmarked field, he could see Natalia.

There were more helicopters and helicopter pilots to ground—permanently—and he had to be about his business.

The knife up his sleeve again, Rourke started for the next machine — and the next pilot.

Chapter Twenty-Three

The arrangement of the Soviet helicopters on the landing field had been perforce random, the unevenness of the field itself dictating that there be no formation. With few exceptions, it was impossible for someone near one craft to have a perfect view of another.

Advantages.

As Rourke walked toward the fifth pilot he was prepared to kill, he realized full well his luck couldn't last forever. And this pilot had one of the new assault rifles.

Disadvantages.

"What is it you want, corporal?"

John Rourke flashed a grin. "A message from the comrade major, comrade captain."

"You can stand there and give me the message, corporal — I have never seen your face before." The man swung the assault rifle into position, the distance still too great for Rourke to use his knife.

"I'd better tell you the truth, then." John Rourke nodded, stopping in his tracks.

"Speak."

"I'm more than five hundred years old and I thought I killed the last of you bastards five centuries ago when the sky caught fire — just came back to finish the job."

"Five centuries—like the comrade colonel—you are—"

The man's eyes flickered. Rourke's stomach churned.

Rourke's right hand stabbed the assault rifle forward as he threw himself down and right, rolling onto his back, then onto his chest. The pilot's assault rifle opened up, chunks of the concrete runway surface thrown skyward. Rourke's right index finger jerked back on the Soviet assault rifle's trigger—an almost total absence of felt recoil, the cyclic rate higher than Rourke had anticipated. At least six shots got off, the muzzle belching a neat tongue of orange fire. The Soviet captain's body twitched, doubled forward, then crashed back, hitting the runway surface, rolling once, spread-eagled face down.

Rourke was up, to his feet, running. Five choppers he had disabled—another five Natalia had taken out. One each he and Natalia would steal—five would be left unless they could be taken out before they got off the ground.

Rourke reached the helicopter, throwing the Soviet assault rifle inside, jumping after it, ducking his head as he ran forward—a technician. The man turned from the control panel. He stared at Rourke. The man wore a corporal's rank as did Rourke. "What is wrong, comrade?"

"Did you make the repairs?" Rourke asked him.

"Only a loose grounding wire—it is fixed—she is ready to fly." The technician smiled happily.

Rourke's left fist snapped out, toward the technician's jawline. Rourke muttered, "Thanks for the quick service."

Rourke's hand connected squarely against the technician's jaw.

"Why did you do that, comrade?" the technician asked, rising closer to his full height — the technician was very tall.

"Ahh." Rourke nodded.

The technician was also very fast, Rourke realized. The man's right flicked out. Rourke jerked his head back and away from it but not fast enough. The man's fist impacted Rourke's jaw on the left side near the base. Rourke stumbled back along the fuselage toward the open sliding doorway, the knife gone from where he'd carried it up his sleeve.

Rourke sprawled against the fuselage floor, his balance gone.

He started to move but the technician was beside him in what seemed like a single stride. The man's hand grabbed at him but Rourke's right fist hammered forward into the abdomen. The technician still smiled, his body not reacting. The man's arms shoved out, the hands opening, thrusting outward from the chest like a basketball player's. Rourke felt himself flying, out of the aircraft, tucking his elbows against his sides, pulling his legs up, trying to impact the runway surface in a roll. Rourke felt the runway surface crash toward him, and he rolled, on his knees, up to his feet, his jaw feeling the numbness. The technician bounded from the open fuselage doorway.

Less than two yards apart, Rourke looked at the man — he was at least seven feet tall. The technician's body looked to have been poured into the fatigue uniform with his muscles rippling visibly under it.

"Vitamins?" Rourke asked him.

The technician smiled, hurling himself forward. John Rourke sidestepped but not fast enough to get in a kick to the groin or anywhere else vital. Rourke twisted half right instead, his left fist hammering out and down as the Soviet technician's body lurched past him. Rourke's knuckles ached with the impact. The technician's body deflected from its flight path and hit the concrete, sprawling. The technician waited there an instant, then pushed himself up in a perfect one hand push-up, bounding to his feet.

"Not often a guy your size is so fast," Rourke told the technician in English.

"Very much, thank you." The man smiled, his English heavily accented.

"Anytime." Rourke nodded. The big man threw himself forward again. Rourke realized he was trapped between the aircraft fuselage and his opponent. Rourke dropped, rolling, under the fuselage, onto his knees, up then, the aircraft between them now.

There was gunfire. Natalia and Paul Rubenstein ran across the field, Natalia pushing the handcart which was loaded with the crates of air to air and air to ground missiles, one of the liberated assault rifles blazing from her right hand.

Rubenstein—the Schmeisser in his right fist, under his left arm a metal ammo box, his left fist closed on the handle of a second box.

"John!"

"I'm takin' this machine—you and Natalia get airborne!"

Rourke wheeled, feeling the rush of air, the huge technician's massive fist rocketing toward him.

Rourke tried to block the man's other hand cutting under the block but Rourke felt the impact against his abdomen and doubled forward. But the technician screamed with pain.

The technician fell back. Rourke dropped to his knees, his wind gone. The man's fist had connected with one of the twin stainless Detonics pistols Rourke had under his uniform blouse, Rourke realized.

The big man's left foot snapped out but Rourke looked up just in time. A stream of curses — Russian — issued from the man's mouth. Rourke's hands caught the big man's foot. Rourke went with its direction of motion, rolling, dragging the man down.

Rourke fell back, losing the foot, his right hand going for the Stechkin, never making it. The big man got to his knees, his fast right hammering out, Rourke taking the impact, falling back, the Stechkin falling from his right hand.

The man hurtled himself forward from his knees, Rourke twisting his body left across the runway surface. If the big man crashed down on him, Rourke realized he'd never get up again. The technician's body slapped hard, arms spread wide, against the concrete. Rourke shifted his own weight on his palms, his left leg snapping out, the flat of his foot in the borrowed Soviet combat boots impacting the right side of the smiling giant's face. Rourke kicked again. A groaning sound. Rourke shifted his weight again, wheeling, his right foot kicking out, missing as the technician rolled away, blood streaming from the right side of the massive man's mouth.

Rourke edged back, half to his feet as the technician, on his knees, swung his left. Rourke dodged his head back, the technician's left fist just glancing off Rourke's chin. Rourke's own left hammered out, crossbody against the right temple of the technician, the man's head snapping back. Rourke's right hooked up, under the chin, the head snapping back again.

Rourke threw himself forward from his knees, his left shoulder impacting the center of the giant's chest, his left shoulder suddenly aching, but the man toppled back with Rourke on top of him.

Rourke realized what he did in the next split second was critical—the man had the bulk and the speed to roll over with Rourke on top of him, to pin Rourke beneath him and kill him.

Rourke's right fist was hammering down toward the Adam's apple, to kill—but Rourke stopped. He drew his right back again, lacing it across the giant man's mouth, then his left, then his right, his left, his right. Rourke's knuckles were bleeding, his fists numbing as he hammered at the man again and again.

The head sagged, lolling to the left side.

Rourke fell back away from the man, gunfire all around them now. Rourke stumbled to his feet, picking up the Stechkin, thrusting it into the flap holster, starting around to the side of the fuselage with the open doorway. He felt it—in the hair on the back of his neck.

John Rourke sidestepped, shifting his weight as he wheeled. The Soviet technician, the lower half of his face smeared crimson with blood, lunged for him. Rourke's right leg was up, making a wide arc, a whooshing sound, the inner side of Rourke's right foot striking the left side of the giant's head, the head snapping right. Rourke's right foot went down,

Rourke shifting his balance, wheeling, back kicking, his left foot hammering against the Soviet technician's chest, Rourke wheeling, the man's body rocking, swaying, Rourke balling both fists together, swinging with them as if they held an invisible baseball bat, throwing his body into it, his feet leaving the ground as both locked-together fists made their impact, Rourke's body shuddering suddenly, a chill running along his spine.

He was falling, his hands going out, breaking his fall as he rolled out of it.

John Rourke snapped his head left — the giant was down, eyes closed, the chest heaving upward and downward, blood washing down the jaw and onto the neck and across the uniform blouse.

Rourke climbed to his feet, sagging against the helicopter fuselage, the gunfire loud now from all sides. He stared at the seven foot tall Soviet technician. "Best fight I've had in years." John started toward the other side of the fuselage — he could barely close his fists and his knuckles streamed blood.

Chapter Twenty-Four

Blood spouted from his knuckles as Rourke closed his fists on the controls of the state-of-the-art Soviet helicopter, the video displays appearing on the screens before him, printed words in Cyrillic alphabet flashing across the screen as the purring of the turbines grew steadily louder. He started memorizing the positioning of the readouts — air speed indicator, altimeter, fuel consumption. But on another level of his mind, John Rourke watched as the black-clad KGB personnel began filling the field, racing toward the machine he occupied, toward the machine Natalia and Paul Rubenstein had commandeered, running in a wedge, assault rifle fire blazing, but the bullet-resistant material that formed the bubble surrounding him absorbed the hits.

He had no idea what acceptable oil pressure and temperature readings would be, no idea what level of RPMs had to be reached — with no gauges to read from but readouts instead. It would be guesswork only.

Already, one of the five helicopters neither he nor Natalia had gotten the chance to destroy was skimming the ground, heading toward Natalia's ship.

Rourke gambled, starting airborne, the ship lurching, swaying left mere inches over the surface of the field — machine guns. Rourke thought he had found the controls, a new display panel lighting. The weapons systems panel. He wheeled the chopper ninety degrees to port, overcompensating, the machine shuddering, lurching downward, Rourke giving the main rotor more power, the ship climbing. Rourke's left thumb flipped the cover at the top of the control wheel, his left hand only gripping the yoke, his right hand working to adjust the mixture, his left thumb depressing the fire control button at the top of the yoke, chunks of the airfield ripping up in a wave as if some invisible plow propelled by a maniac coursed across it. He started the chopper climbing, leveling off at less than fifty feet over the runway surface, more accurate machine gun fire pouring toward him from the one already airborne Soviet machine.

Rourke pressed the fire control button again, the helicopter that attacked him veering hard starboard and climbing.

Natalia's machine was airborne as well now, Rubenstein visible in the open fuselage doorway, one of the Soviet assault rifles in each hand now, both weapons firing toward the Soviet personnel on the ground.

Natalia's machine turned almost three hundred and sixty degrees—there was a puff of off-white smoke, then a bleached white contrail—one of the still unsabotaged Soviet choppers exploded, a fireball of yellow and black belching skyward. Rourke cut his own machine one hundred and eighty degrees, then started to climb, finding his missile controls, the display panel activated—a targeting computer as well. Rourke found the switch to override it. As he hit the override switch, Natalia's machine opened fire on the already airborne machine, a miss, the Soviet-manned chopper turning one hundred eighty degrees, to fire. Hitting the override switch had lost him the control panel.

Rourke punched up the missile control panel, again, scanning the control readouts, to override the targeting computer and fire on manual. Instead of hitting the override switch, he hit the switch marked manual—the targeting computer was off now—at least he assumed that it was, but the control panel was still illuminated. Sighting via the control panel, he lined up his starboard forward missile bank on the Soviet chopper now pursuing Natalia and Paul Rubenstein. The Soviet pilot was banking hard, following Natalia's craft as she strafed another of the machines still on the ground. It was her superior knowledge of Russian, Rourke realized, that had allowed her to command the chopper so well—she was equally as good a pilot as he.

But the miss she had made with her missile had been due to the targeting computer—the Soviet pilot would have known how to outfly it for just such a contingency should a machine fall into enemy hands.

The Soviet pilot's machine was closing now, Natalia banking away from it, making another strafing run, knocking out at least a half dozen of the KGB troopers firing at her from the airfield. Rourke activated the firing interlock, his left hand over the fire control mechanism, his eyes flickering from the control panel—it looked like a video game—to the living target he wished to destroy.

The enemy helicopter was under his sights—Rourke hit the firing mechanism.

The image of the enemy gunship seemed to flare on the screen as Rourke looked away, the enemy chopper a ball of flame now, still airborne, but falling, crashing downward toward the gunships still on the ground and the men firing from cover surrounding them.

Rourke activated his radio switch. "Natalia — come in."

"John — you got him!"

"Let's get the hell out of here — follow me — Rourke out." Rourke throttled out the main rotor, feeling himself pressed back into the pilot's seat by the sudden acceleration — the new gunship was fast.

A half dozen of them, possibly less, could pace out the returning Eden Project fleet as they started their landing patterns, pace out the Eden Project fleet and destroy it.

Behind him, as he looked back once, the airfield was a sea of flames.

Chapter Twenty-Five

Helmut Sturm stood on the ground, despite the swirling sands around him, through his goggles peering skyward—the main armada of the Condor Squadron gunships was coming from the southwest, and the sight of it filled him with pride. His right hand rested on the full flap holster at his right hip—the gun carried there was an antique, from another war, another age. It was the Walther P-38 9mm his ancestor had carried throughout the Second World War in the service of the Third Reich. It was still functional, and he had the ammunition custom made in one of the weapons workshops—he could drive tacks with it.

There was one other relic of his ancestor, and he had left this with Helene, for one of their sons to possess, to cherish. It was an Iron Cross, presented to Helmut Sturm's ancestor by Adolf Hitler himself.

Helmut Sturm had witnessed an eclipse of the sun, and today again the sun eclipsed.

No moon passed between it and the Earth, but the ground was in shadow and the sky above seemed dark as night.

Overhead now, the Condor Squadron gunships, one hundred strong, the winds generated by their combined rotor blades tearing at his clothing, at his flesh, the sound of the wind and not the silenced helicopters like a shrieking howl now, his subordinates surrounding him, equally battered by the wind and the sand.

Helmut Sturm began to walk, his own machine on the ground, the eclipse passing as the one hundred gunships passed on toward the northeast.

A force moved ahead of them, a force that did not register on their radar screens, a force of considerably lesser size than their own—an advance guard had seen it disappear beyond a mountain range, the force flying low, as if skimming the ground—did it, too, search for life? The massive cargo aircraft had been seen on radar. They had brought these strange ships, Sturm thought, and left them here.

Invaders? He smiled—one invader now pursued another, the prize the North American continent.

But who these invaders were—it remained a mystery. Perhaps some surviving Americans to reclaim what once had been theirs five centuries earlier. Or perhaps the Russians, come to claim what they could out of the destruction they had wrought.

He boarded his machine, his uniform thick with sand, his goggles coated with it—his black machine coated with it.

But to have seen what he had seen—the power of National Socialism obscuring the sun.

If his commander asked, he would contrive a reason for it—unless his commander could already guess.

"Pilot—we must be under way."

Inside himself, he murmured, "Destiny awaits."

The machine began to rise.

Chapter Twenty-Six

"Helicopters — holy shit!" Michael Rourke cursed himself as well — he had left the double action .44 Magnums in the camouflaged-painted Ford pickup truck. Slung across his back was the Stalker, the smaller Magnum Sales counterpart, the Predator, in the crossdraw holster between his navel and left hipbone. He started to run, glancing behind him and skyward — they were coming out of the sunset, dozens of them, all but obscuring the sunset as they came.

The Stalker unslung from his back, he wheeled, leveling the scoped, long-barreled stainless Ruger single action — could they be friendly? Was firing at them starting something that might not start otherwise?

He hesitated.

Then the sand near his feet churned as if struck by an invisible plow shaft — a long, long explosive sound filled the air, and there was a cracking sound — again more of the sand, this time nearer to him, blew upward and outward.

The nearest of the choppers was two hundred yards, and Michael Rourke swung the Stalker on line, sighting through the 2X Leupold Silver scope. The fuselage would be armored. The bubble dome would be bullet resistant. But these were his very special handloads, an increased powder charge backing a three hundred grain bullet. His right thumb cocked the hammer, and he settled the scope on the bubble dome of the lead black helicopter. Michael Rourke triggered the shot, the Stalker bucking hard into the web of his hand, the muzzle climbing — but the lead helicopter immediately began to bank, steeply, rising suddenly, more gunfire pounding the sand around him as Michael Rourke started running again — he had hit the machine, inflicted some damage. The Stalker clenched tight in his right fist, he threw himself into the run toward the trucks and the bulldozer.

"The generator — cut the generator so they can't see our lights!" He shouted over the sound of the gunfire, over the wind that beat around and behind him, clouds of sand rising in waves on each side of him now as he ran on, the helicopter gunships strangely silent in operation. Whose were they? He guessed inside himself that somehow the clue to their identity lay in the identity of the downed pilot and whatever mysterious aircraft he had flown, the downed pilot whose trail had led him into the cannibal camp, led him to find Madison and save her, Madison, the girl who was now his wife in every way but ceremony, the girl who carried his child in her — they both felt that.

He kept running.

He could see Annie coming out of the shelter, strapping her gunbelt to her waist as the tent flap opened again and Madison exited the tent behind her. "Run for it — run —"

Gunfire again, a burning feeling that consumed his body, then a numbness in his legs and arms — as his body pitched forward, he could see Annie firing her Scoremaster skyward toward the advancing machines — he wanted to shout to her that it was useless, but his mouth wouldn't work, and he tasted sand against his lips and on his tongue, and sand rippled along the ground on both sides of him and he closed his eyes.

Chapter Twenty-Seven

There had been no pursuit and John Rourke had decided to hell with caution and taken the most direct route toward the encampment in southern Georgia near the highway which would serve as a landing strip for the Eden Project fleet. Throughout the flight—in the jet-powered helicopters it had consumed three hours—he had flexed his fingers so his hands would still work properly, the pain increasing in the aftermath of the fight with the giant Soviet technician.

Rourke throttled down, checking the air speed indicator, talking into his headset microphone. "I'm going to the same frequency as the Beechcraft—we're only a few miles away and maybe Michael or Annie'll pick us up. You do the same, Natalia—Rourke out."

"Roger on that—Natalia out." Rourke punched the right keys, the frequency numbers appearing in red digital readout on the communications console. Static, as if the frequency were open.

"This is John Rourke, come in base, over."

Static only.

"Annie—Michael—we're on the way home—may have some company after a while but all's well for the moment—come back. Over."

Static only.

"Hey—this is Dad—let's hear from you, over."

Natalia's voice, "John—let me try—Natalia to

base — Natalia to base — come in, over."

And then a voice — it echoed in Rourke's earphone. "Natalia — after all these years, that voice — it still excites me. And Dr. Rourke — the memories your voice bring back — "

There was silence on the radio, then Natalia's voice. "Vladmir."

Rourke licked his lips.

Over the radio set now, all John Rourke heard was laughter, insane laughter.

Chapter Twenty-Eight

John Rourke's hands shook. There had been a portable transceiver aboard the helicopter and in his left hand he held this now, the frequency open to the second Soviet chopper which hovered in the near daylight-bright moonlight less than a quarter mile away from where Rourke had landed. Natalia and Paul Rubenstein were aboard the second craft.

There had been no more of the transmission from Vladmir Karamatsov—the man John Rourke had thought he had killed five centuries ago, the man who had been Natalia's husband, the man who had nearly killed her, almost beaten her to death before she had resisted.

In John Rourke's right hand was the Soviet assault rifle. He still wore the Soviet uniform, but his twin stainless Detonics pistols were exposed now, tucked between the black fatigue uniform's trousers and blouse. His own clothes were aboard the second helicopter—Rubenstein had brought them.

He called into the moonlight, "Michael—Annie—Sarah! Sarah!"

There was no answer.

He kept walking, toward the tent, toward the Ford pickup truck, toward the other vehicles. The earth mover was silent. The landing strip nearly completely through—Michael had made the work go more quickly than Rourke had anticipated possible.

"Sarah!"

Rourke swallowed hard. "Kurinami! Dr. Halverson!"

A voice from the transceiver in his left hand, "John — what's —"

"Nothing, Paul — how's Natalia. Over."

"She's flyin' the chopper — she hasn't said a word. Over."

"Stay by the radio, Paul — Rourke out."

He kept walking, shouting, "Madison — Michael — answer me!"

There was no answer.

John Rourke stopped before the tent flap.

He swallowed hard again.

There was no light from inside the tent. "Inside — anybody there?"

Rourke propped the tent flap with the muzzle of the Soviet rifle, catching the flap's edge on the front sight assembly, pulling the flap outward.

John Rourke stepped inside — darkness.

A flashlight from the Soviet chopper — Rourke jammed the radio transceiver into his left hip pocket, taking the flashlight from the pocket, flicking it on.

John Rourke swept the beam across the tent floor to the far side.

In a chair, his trousers drenched with blood, his shirt saturated with it, his face white like death was his son.

John Rourke dropped the flashlight, watching the light as it rolled across the tent floor, his shaking left hand finding the radio transceiver, raising it close to his lips. "This is John Rourke."

"John — what — "

"Stay off, Paul — Karamatsov — do you hear me? Do you hear me — Karamatsov!"

Rourke screamed the name.

"Yes." There was only laughter then.

John Rourke depressed the push-to-talk button. "This time, motherfucker — I'll rip your guts out with my bare hands and burn them so you can never come back."

Over the radio, there was only laughter.

Chapter Twenty-Nine

She watched John Rourke's eyes — sweat beaded around them and she took the folded bandana handkerchief and wiped his brow and daubed near his eyes. She watched John Rourke's hands — rubber gloved, stained red with the blood of his nearly dead son whose life he was trying to save.

She had no doubt that John Rourke would save Michael Rourke — if anyone could. He had saved her life — surgically and otherwise.

It was because of the otherwise part, as she considered, that she looked toward the tent flap and called out to Paul Rubenstein, "Paul — come inside, please."

The tent flap opened after a moment. "What is it?"

"I have something I must do — you don't need to guard from outside — my husband won't be coming yet — if at all. He knows what to expect. And so do I — you attend John. Give him the help he needs — go scrub — you know how — he taught us both."

"Forget that," Rourke rasped.

"Paul — you had better do as I say — or otherwise John won't have help for a few critical moments — I have to leave —"

"Bullshit," Rourke hissed, not looking at her.

"What are you talking about?" Paul Rubenstein asked.

"I have someone to meet —"

"They've got Annie and Sarah, they've got Madison—and maybe she's got my grandchild in her. They've got Kurinami and Halverson—they're not getting you."

"They haven't got anyone, John—it's Vladmir. And there are only two people Vladmir would allow close enough to him to kill him—you and me."

John Rourke looked up from Michael's right kidney. "Paul—she tries leaving here kneecap her if you have to—"

"What—hey—"

"Do it," Rourke shouted, looking again at his surgery.

"I love you very deeply, Paul—you are my finest friend—don't make me hurt you—"

"Talk about ego deflating." Rubenstein smiled. "Look—we'll get Michael patched up and then we'll all go after Karamatsov and get everyone back and take care of—"

"John must attend his son—or Michael will die. After that, someone will need to be with Michael constantly while John flies one of the helicopters to destroy the bridges so the Space Shuttles can land. One of the two of you will have to work the earth mover to clear the debris—Michael can't be left alone. That leaves me."

She had spoken to Paul Rubenstein, but she looked now at John Rourke. "I won't let you go," John Rourke told her, his voice cold. lifeless sounding to her.

"I love you, too. But Paul, try as he might—he couldn't stop me without killing me and he would never do that. And you can't lay down your surgical

116

instruments to stop me without killing your only son. I'm leaving."

"Paul!"

"Hey, look — Natal —" Her left hand flashed forward — to his windpipe. A short duration pinch, his hands reaching up to her hand, then her right hand applying downward pressure to his left side to temporarily interrupt the flow of blood in the subclavian artery — his body sagged to its knees and she cushioned his head with her hands as she rested it on the floor of the tent.

"He should be awake in a few moments, John — and a few moments after that and he'll be good as new."

"Natalia — you —"

She rested Paul's head, standing, walking over to the improvised operating table and taking John Rourke's face in her hands. She pulled down the mask that covered his mouth and nose and kissed him hard on the lips. "I never loved any other human being like you — I've made love with you in my mind since the first moment I saw you, John — you've ravished my body in my dreams like you filled my soul in reality." She touched her lips to his again — his hands were full of his son's blood and he didn't touch her, could not touch her. She raised the surgical mask.

She started to walk away. "Natalia — I'll find another —"

"No, you won't find another way, John," she said, stopping, looking at him.

"I love you — you can't —"

"That's why I can." She looked at John Rourke once more and walked out through the tent flap and into the bright moonlight. She began stripping off her pistol belt—she would not need her guns and someone else could use them—perhaps John would keep them as a remembrance of her. She reached the Ford pickup, set the gunbelt on the seat beside Michael's unused guns. Sarah's gun, Annie's gun, the stock Government Model Colt .45 of Dr. Halverson, Kurinami's identical pistol, Michael's .44 Magnum single action Rugers, all the M-16s—she could see them neatly set out in the truck bed. Vladmir had left them as a sign of contempt, she knew.

They had been useless against him.

She reached into the hip pocket of her black jumpsuit—the Bali-Song knife. It came alive in her hand—the clicking sound of it opening, closing, opening again, like a butterfly folding and unfolding its wings.

It was childish, but she inverted the knife in her hand and stabbed it into the top of the Ford's dashboard, leaving it there, the handle halves closing around it.

She stared at the night sky, starting to walk toward her helicopter—while John had prepared Michael for surgery, she had emptied the gunship of all armament. She needed transportation only.

To death.

Natalia Anastasia Tiemerovna, major, Committee For State Security of The Soviet, told the moonlight, "I am coming, Vladmir—and I will have to do."

She kept walking, wishing for a cigarette.

Chapter Thirty

She spoke into the headset microphone: "This is Major Tiemerovna—talk me in to your position—I wish to converse privately with my husband—over."

"Comrade major, we have you on radar—course correction adjustments to follow—stand by on this frequency, out."

She stared ahead—the moonlight was nearly dead. It would be many hours before John Rourke had concluded the operation to save his son's life. Multiple projectile wounds near both kidneys. Fifty-nine hours had passed, sixty-four hours plus or minus one hour remaining until the Eden Project fleet would have to land.

It was evident to her how Vladmir Karamatsov had known where to find them. He had received radio transmissions outlining what had happened near the site of the Womb, projected their course and beat them to their destination.

He had anticipated Michael would be dead—that both herself and John Rourke would come to him.

She closed her eyes for an instant, thanking God that Michael had only been wounded, not for Michael's sake, but for John's sake—that John had not lost his son and that John had been, because of his son's condition, powerless to prevent her actions.

The radio came alive again, giving the course correction, and she set her instruments accordingly, mechanically wondering how it would be—would he attempt to kill her instantly?

She anticipated now—that he would torture her, make her beg for death. That would perhaps give her the time she needed—to free Sarah, Annie, Madison, and the others, and then to kill him.

And it would have to be done quickly, to prevent her husband from having the time to once again attack the camp where John now labored to save his son's life, to prevent Col. Vladmir Karamatsov from killing John and Paul and if Michael lived, undoing Michael's father's work.

"I have the coordinates," she said into the headset. "ETA twenty minutes. I shall expect to be met—Major Tiemerovna out." She knew perfectly well that she would be.

She knew her destination—the mountains of Northeastern Georgia, very close to the Retreat itself. More of her husband's sense of drama.

Chapter Thirty-One

Natalia Anastasia Tiemerovna stood before her helicopter, an officer and two assault rifle-armed enlisted personnel running toward her. She watched them, her hands on her hips. She recognized the officer—Captain Popovski.

Popovski, tall, thin, young—despite the five centuries since she had seen him last—snapped to attention and saluted her. "Comrade Major Tiemerovna!"

She nodded, not returning the red-haired man's salute. She had given her last salute to valiant Russians centuries ago and would not sully its meaning now. "Captain—you look well, I seem to remember that you smoked—you do not still, do you?"

"Yes, comrade major—I am ashamed to admit that I do."

"May I have a cigarette?"

"Yes, comrade major—we make some few cigarettes—they are like American cigarettes were, I think." He extended a silver cigarette case and Natalia reached into it, taking one of the cigarettes. "Corporal—the comrade major's cigarette!"

The corporal to Popovski's right stepped forward quickly, his rifle swinging pendulum fashion at his side—he ignited a stick match and she heard the rising and falling sound, smelled the sulfur as it flickered and burned. She stabbed the end of the cigarette into the flame—it was not like American cigarette but satisfactory. She promised herself that if somehow she lived, she would smoke through at least a package of the cigarettes at the Retreat—and she would then quit again. "Thank you, corporal." She smiled at him, holding back her laughter as he stared at her. He dropped the match as it burned his fingertips.

He stomped the match on the ground beneath the sunrising shadows of the mountains around them and stepped back to stand behind and beside Captain Popovski. "I wish to see my husband, Colonel Karamatsov—he still calls himself colonel? Not marshall or something?"

"The comrade colonel is interested in seeing the comrade major as well." Popovski nodded—grimly, she thought.

"I'm sure he is." She nodded, inhaling the cigarette smoke deeply this time—she coughed. For five hundred years she had not smoked.

"If you would come this way, comrade major—" Popovski began to walk beside her, gesturing them up from the relatively flat valley floor and into the rocks. She walked ahead, Popovski to her left and slightly behind her. "Comrade major—I only inquire to know the strength of our enemy—"

"Your enemy," Natalia corrected.

"Yes, comrade major—but the man the comrade colonel left behind in the chair—the man bled badly and—"

"He lives." She looked at Popovski and thought she saw the flicker of a smile in his eyes. He nodded, saying nothing. "Your new gunships are quite advanced."

"I wish that I had the abilities to fly one of the machines, comrade major."

"Perhaps, someday." She smiled, looking toward the tents set along the base of the mountain she approached. One was larger than all the others, centrally located. It would be her husband's tent. "The prisoners—the prisoners my husband took after the young man was shot—they are well, Popovski?"

"Yes, comrade major—the young woman with the very long hair—"

"Yes?"

"She required three men to subdue her." He looked down at his feet.

Natalia let herself smile. She would not identify Annie as Annie—her husband might wish to torture and kill anyone named Rourke. She asked the question of Popovski. "What has he planned for me?"

Popovski stopped.

Natalia stopped.

Popovski answered her in English. "You should not have come, comrade major—he does horrible things to women—there are wild tribes in Europe and he takes their women and beats them to death and rapes them and—"

"What has he planned for me?" Natalia asked again.

"I do not know, comrade major—but you would be wise to kill yourself first."

"I cannot—I brought no weapons."

His eyes flickered for a moment—across her body. She could feel them. "I am sorry, comrade major—truly. Were there a God, I would pray to him for you."

"I have discovered something most amazing, Andre—there is a God. And thank you." Natalia Tiemerovna walked toward the large tent.

Chapter Thirty-Two

He had felt like this once before in his life, Paul Rubenstein thought, watching the sun rise. He had felt like this when the realization that New York was gone and so was the girl to whom he had been engaged, the girl he had told that he loved was gone as well.

Paul Rubenstein saw Annie Rourke's face in his mind as he watched the rising sun. Had Karamatsov killed her? Or had he done worse? Rubenstein knew Col. Vladmir Karamatsov well by reputation.

Natalia had spoken of what Karamatsov had done to her—that night they had shared a fire's warmth in the middle of a blizzard.

And now Natalia, too, was lost to him—as though Karamatsov were some devil who could not die. Paul Rubenstein himself had watched through the scope of Rourke's Steyr-Mannlicher SSG as Rourke had faced him down, shot him. Rubenstein shivered—had he not been too level-headed (he told himself that) he would have believed there really was some supernatural quality to Karamatsov's existence.

And Michael—John Rourke had removed seven bullets from his son's back, one of the bullets very close to the spine, two of the bullets nearly penetrating the right kidney. The loss of blood was the greatest enemy—Rourke had given two pints of his own blood to his son and been so weak that Rubenstein had been

125

forced, under John Rourke's direction, to finish closing the incisions.

Michael rested now, but could not be moved.

John Rourke had fallen into an exhausted sleep.

Paul Rubenstein alternatively watched the wounded man — Michael — and the horizon, for another attack.

He was powerless to attempt to rescue Annie, or Sarah, or any of the others.

When John Rourke awakened, before any plans could be laid, the bridges would have to be blown and the improvised runway surface cleared.

And at any moment Karamatsov might attack.

The majority of the sand had already been cleared — but the bridges. Would Karamatsov wait until the six craft of the Eden Project fleet were in the landing process, then attack and shoot them down?

Rubenstein shivered again — lack of sleep, lack of knowing what to do, forced inaction.

Fear, but not for himself.

Without blood, Michael's recovery would be slow at best. Without John Rourke, should one of the wounds become infected, Michael would die.

"Damnit," Paul Rubenstein whispered to the sunrise. He clenched the Schmeisser tighter in his fists.

Chapter Thirty-Three

Sarah Rourke, her wrists bleeding, had twisted her left hand finally so that she could touch at the knot. "All these guys must have spent five hundred years learning how to tie ropes tight," she whispered, staring at Elaine Halverson.

They had been placed in the tent so long ago that Sarah Rourke had lost count of the hours, hands and ankles tied, gags tied in their mouths, hands tethered to stakes driven deep into the rocky ground beneath the tent.

Annie had not opened her eyes—the place where the rifle butt had impacted her jaw was darkening, purple now. Madison only stared. But Madison had been a good girl, Sarah reflected, trying to defend Annie after Annie had been subdued, trying to block the blow of the rifle butt—but unsuccessfully.

Kurinami's face reflected his struggle as well, the young Japanese naval aviator requiring more than a half dozen of the KGB assault troops to be subdued, then Kurinami, hands and feet held by a man per limb, had been beaten in the face and the abdomen. His lips were puffy, dried blood accumulated under the mouth and along the line of his jaw on the left side, his left eye half closed and blackened. But Kurinami as well had been working on his ropes. Sarah had watched him.

Elaine Halverson had emptied her pistol, then clawed with her nails at one of her attackers, but an assault rifle pressed against her head had forced her surrender. Sarah shrugged, remembering—some people fought in different ways. Elaine Halverson, too, had been fighting the ropes which bound her.

"Michael," Sarah Rourke whispered. The handkerchief that had been used as a gag wet from her own saliva now sagged below her chin.

Sarah Rourke was the only one of them who had worked her gag free.

But Elaine Halverson had worked hers nearly free, rubbing her chin against the rock surface beneath her, the woman's chin rubbed raw of skin in spots and bleeding. Sarah Rourke spoke again. "If John hasn't come for us by now, that must mean Michael was still alive and John is working to save him. We may have help coming in any event—Paul or Natalia."

Elaine Halverson was finally free of the gag, leaning up, choking for an instant. Coughing still, she whispered, "Natalia—but this madman Karamatsov—he's—he's her—"

"I know he's her husband. John thought he had killed Karamatsov before the holocaust—Michael told me about it. But it doesn't matter—"

"I—I didn't think—"

"That I liked Natalia? You've seen it—she's in love with my husband. My husband's in love with her—but I don't question the fact she's on our side. Karamatsov tried killing her once—almost beat her to death. He's an animal. And anyway—she loves John—if she'd wanted me out of the way, I wouldn't be here. She's the one who prepared the injections when we took the cry-

128

ogenic sleep. She helped John find me and find the children — she's ahh — well, she is — but if John hasn't gotten here by now, that means Paul or Natalia or both of them will be on the way. But we might not have the time —" and Sarah tugged at the knot, breaking one of her already short nails, but the knot loosened. "Might not have the time to wait. It must be morning by now."

Sarah Rourke began working on the next part of the knot, having no idea if there were more knots to undo. She kept working. And a smile crossed her lips — a Rourke didn't give up.

Chapter Thirty-Four

His face was drawn and his hands looked swollen — Paul Rubenstein watched John Rourke as Rourke stepped from the tent. The familiar double Alessi shoulder rig carrying the twin stainless Detonics pistols was across his shoulders, the flap holster with the Metalifed and Mag-Na-Ported six-inch Colt Python at his right hip, on his left hip one of the long-bladed Gerber MkII fighting knives, the most recent permanent addition to John Rourke's armament.

For some reason, Paul Rubenstein felt compelled to stand. "How is Michael?"

"He's very weak — but I can't do anything about that beyond what I've done. I can't transfuse any more blood to him and still be functional myself. That Karamatsov didn't smash the radio set means he wants the Eden Project to land — so he can use those choppers to shoot them down. That's why he hasn't attacked again. I'm half surprised he didn't blow down those bridges for us just to speed it up. Because that's what I've got to do. I'm getting that Russian chopper airborne," Rourke almost whispered, lighting one of the thin dark tobacco cigars he habitually smoked, his eyes masked behind the dark lenses of his sunglasses. "I'll blow the bridges with some of the missiles, then take the pickup truck from the supply cache and head after Natalia, try to spring Sarah and Annie and Madison and the others, try to keep Natalia from getting killed. You'll have to work the earth mover—bulldoze the debris clear from the highway, then signal the shuttles to land. I already used the radio, told Commander Dodd what had happened. They have some other airborne activity—it's in Alabama—maybe more of the Russians, I don't know. I can't worry about it, either. They have to land—we get them down a little sooner all the better for Michael. They have plasma aboard and some of the fleet's compliment had the same blood type as Michael. Sarah has the same blood type, and so does Annie. Whatever happens, we're giving Michael a chance."

Paul Rubenstein looked at his friend. "I wish I were going with you."

"I wish you were, too—but what you've got to do here is more important. I've gotta finish the job I started five centuries ago. If I'd put a single bullet through his brain, none of this would have happened—Karamatsov would have been dead. I should have planned ahead." John Rourke studied the tip of his cigar, Rubenstein watching him. "But I won't make the same mistake again."

Rourke started toward the helicopter.

Chapter Thirty-Five

When she had entered the tent, Vladmir Karamatsov had simply stared at her and she had stood before his desk, waiting. It had been a full ten minutes — she had left her Rolex with her other things that perhaps Annie could use, or Madison — as she had reckoned it in her head.

Finally, he had raised the pistol from his desk top and pointed it at her face and very quietly told her, "Undress, Natalia."

She had closed her eyes and begun — slowly, because she knew that was how he wanted it — to strip her clothes from her body.

The boots were gone now as were the black leather gloves she had worn and on the tent floor beside them, the one-piece black jumpsuit. She balanced herself as she removed first the left, then the right black boot sock, letting these fall to the floor as well.

She wore nothing but the lace-trimmed, beige silk teddy, and slowly, she edged down first one shoulder strap, then the other, pushing the garment down past her waist and past her hips — her breasts exposed to him. She shuddered. Her whole body exposed to him as she let the teddy fall around her ankles, then stepped out of it and back from it.

She opened her eyes. "Why did you come here willingly?" he asked her.

"To get close enough to you that I can kill you my-self—and end this."

"Even at the cost of your own life—you will never see John Rourke again, Natalia."

"I know that—and yes, at the cost of my own life. Some things are more important than life, Vladmir."

"I agree," he enthused, smiling at her—his eyes held a madness she had seen that night he had beaten her—so many years ago. "For example, pleasure is more important than life, the life of someone else, at least. And for five centuries—even while I slept, do you know that I dreamed of it? But for all those years, I wanted no pleasure more than I wanted to destroy you, just a piece at a time. You won't die—not yet. That would be pointless. I have medical experts who can keep you alive despite the pain, despite—despite all of it. I want to make you beg to die, and then of course I won't let you die—that would ruin it all. But I have experimented ever since my awakening. With whips, clubs, electrodes, hot irons—with all the devices I could think of to cause pain to a woman. If there were still other living creatures besides man on the earth, ahh—there are things I could do to you that would delight me and make you scream until your throat bled with it, until you could never utter another sound, but yet you would still go on screaming." He sighed loudly, then smiled again. "But other things will have to do. And Rourke—he will come for you—and for all the others, whoever they are. I know the one I left for him was his son—no two men could look so alike unless twin brothers or father and son. He played games with the cryogenic chambers, didn't he?"

Natalia nodded.

"One of those two girls is his daughter—never mind telling me now—you'll tell me later. And the woman— that is the legendary Sarah for whom he searched. I'll try her myself and let you know how good the competition was, darling. And the daughter, too—and then many of the men would surely like to have them. And the black woman—a novelty for my men—and perhaps for some of the women, too. And the Japanese— well—we shall let him give us a show. He is very good with the martial arts—we can let him fight to the death—that should be amusing to us all. I'll let you watch while Sarah and Rourke's daughter and the black woman are raped. And the other girl, too—I'll enjoy your reaction. And after weeks of abusing your body and your mind and your very soul, when death is all that you crave, I have devised a most ingenious method—but slow. This new atmosphere of ours. The sun is stronger. I will take you to the height of a great mountain where the sun shines brightly and let your flesh burn and rot from your body while you still live. Something to look forward to, hmm." He smiled again.

She had calculated the distance to the other side of the desk—if she failed, he would kill her. If she succeeded, she would kill him.

She knew that he had calculated it. She threw herself forward, his pistol a blur as it moved upward toward her face, her hands to his neck—her left hand drew back, the heel of it aimed toward the base of his nose. She was screaming, "Die!"

She heard a voice behind her—felt a sudden pain across her back, her body sagging, the blow from the heel of her left hand deflected by her husband's right arm, then pain again at the base of her skull — she was screaming, "Die!" as the blackness and the coldness washed over her.

Chapter Thirty-Six

John Rourke dropped his altitude, coming low toward the bridge so he could fire from the inside of the bridge supports, blowing most of the debris away from the road rather than into it.

Rourke pressed the two fire controls, one missile firing from the port side of the fuselage, another from the tail section, targeted toward the opposite support.

He counted under his breath, reaching three before he was able to go for altitude. At five the concussion from in front of the helicopter and behind it made the machine shudder around him, the controls not responding for an instant, the tail spinning wildly, then full control again, a fireball uncomfortably close, belching skyward, heat from it searing the plexiglass or its more modern equivalent, Rourke throttling out, glancing beneath him once as the fireball separated from its source — the bridge was all but disintegrated.

He followed the course of the road because the shuttle craft would have to follow it on landing, the second bridge already nearly dead ahead. The Soviet gunship responded well enough, but it was not human engineered to his tastes.

He began decelerating, arming another forward and aft missile compliment, ready, the bridge's design something he had long since memorized, could envision in his sleep.

John Rourke's head ached—the forced giving of blood in twice the accepted amount. His hands were stiff, pained when he moved them. But he could still pull a trigger.

Could still kill Karamatsov—this time there would be no mistake.

The second bridge; Rourke flew toward it. In his mind, he thought the word, *fire*, his hand activating the controls—first the forward missile, then the aft, making the chopper climb, throttling out as the explosion roared up behind him.

The helicopter climbed under his hands, Rourke banking, turning the machine a full one hundred eighty degrees—the second bridge, like the first, was no more.

In the distance, Paul Rubenstein already was bring-ing up the earth mover.

John Rourke banked again, dropping altitude to skim over the sand, blowing sand from the highway surface with the rotor downdraft.

The Detonics Scoremasters he had taken from The Place—they already were packed into the pickup truck. His wife's Trapper Scorpion, his daughter's Scoremaster, Halverson's 1911A1, Kurinami's Government Model also, and Natalia's things. The Rolex watch, the Bali-Song knife, the twin Metalife Custom L-Frames.

John Rourke closed his eyes, envisioning Vladmir Karamatsov's face. "Die—son of a bitch—"

Chapter Thirty-Seven

Sarah Rourke tugged — still the knot did not give way.

She looked at Dr. Elaine Halverson — Halverson shrugged. "I can't get it."

She looked past Elaine Halverson — Akiro Kurinami had been sitting upright for some twenty minutes, his legs no longer straight ahead of him. He squatted on his haunches instead, his eyes wide open, staring, as if in a trance, the left eye visibly bloodshot in the light of the propane lamp.

"Akiro," Elaine Halverson began.

But his eyes never flickered.

Sarah Rourke watched, each muscle in Kurinami's legs and arms and chest seeming to ripple under the dirt-stained white jumpsuit he wore, the NASA patch half ripped from it, Kurinami's chest rising and falling more rapidly, his lips drawing back, baring his teeth around the gag, the muscles around his eyes twitching.

"Akiro —"

"No," Sarah Rourke interrupted. "A friend of John's — before the Night of The War — he used to call that summoning up chi —"

"What —"

"He's focusing all his energy, all his strength —"

"To rip apart the ropes?" Elaine Halverson gasped.

"I don't think so — wait —" Sarah Rourke watched.

138

Kurinami's face was going pale — she wondered if it were physically possible for a human being to control blood flow, to divert blood — Kurinami's eyelids flickered and he looked about to faint.

"Akiro—" Elaine Halverson said again, her voice a loud whisper.

Kurinami's entire body seemed to twitch, to half lift from the ground. There was a grinding sound, Kurinami's body snapping up, twisting, wrenching —

He had ripped the spike from the rocky ground in which it had been imbedded, his hands still bound — his wrists streamed blood as he rolled across the floor toward her. The spike was still in his hands.

He looked at her — Sarah Rourke felt herself smile. "You want me to work the knots with my teeth?"

Kurinami, gagged still, grunted something unintelligible, nodding vigorously.

Sarah Rourke smiled again — "Get close to me — Elaine — you work your own knots — hurry."

Kurinami began wriggling into position. Sarah Rourke hoped that someone aboard the Eden Project was a dentist — just in case.

Like a rat gnawing at a barrier, Sarah began chewing at the knots binding Kurinami's wrists.

Chapter Thirty-Eight

One of the induction filters had become clogged from the sand — but the repairs were nearly made and Sturm had agreed with Standarten Führer Mann that having encountered no resistance there was no need to press the advance without rest. The trip up from Argentina had been arduous, on men and equipment.

Helmut Sturm sat now, at the small folding table, a brisk breeze blowing across the sand, Sigfried, his wife's brother, sitting to his right. "Helmut — those aircraft — Americans, do you think?"

"They run ahead of us — whether they run from us or not is another question. But Americans — I think they are not Americans. I think they are Russian. Our historic enemy — Mann was wise indeed to send along the scouting ships to ascertain their destination — and while we rest here, we can prepare ourselves to strike, to destroy them, to crush them. No — all goes well and it is not Americans who pilot these aircraft somewhere out there. It is Russians. And we shall defeat them. We shall conquer."

He looked at his brother-in-law — the younger man nodded, satisfied apparently. Helmut Sturm clapped Sigfried on the back, Sturm rising. "It will be well to be on the move again, yes, Sigfried?"

"Yes, Helmut — to press our enemies — to achieve victory." His brother-in-law was a younger man and did not understand the concept of historic destiny as well as he, Sturm thought. Sigfried was still learning, absorbing.

Sturm understood destiny — it was in the faces of his children, in the proud eyes of his wife when her fingers clasped against the life inside her womb — a master of the Earth.

Sturm found his cap and pulled it on — a walk toward the fringe of the camp, to assay the desert. It was just the thing.

"Come, Sigfried — let us walk, my friend."

The younger man beside him, Helmut Sturm returned the salute of a subordinate as he walked ahead. Soon the scout ships would return — soon it would begin again.

Chapter Thirty-Nine

Manfred sat at the head of the table, as he customarily did when her husband was away with his troops. Helene Sturm felt the kicking of her fifth child inside her womb—perhaps her fifth and sixth. There were the more advanced techniques available now, and she could easily have had it ascertained for certain, even the sexes of the children foretold. But like her own mother, she too preferred to learn these more as she felt nature intended.

"Mother—would you pass the bread, please?" Manfred asked her, looking up from his sausage and smiling.

"Yes." She took the small basket with the sliced rye bread and handed it to her youngest son. "Willy—pass this to your older brother—now quickly." As she handed Wilhelm the basket, the clock chimed.

She looked across the apartment's largest room to the far wall—it was just twelve-thirty. Manfred was looking at her as she turned her eyes back to the table. "What is it, Mother? You appear agitated."

She made herself smile. "It is nothing—but I have an appointment in fifteen minutes—Manfred? Can you see that the rest of the sausage is put away, and the bread and—"

"Where do you go, Mother?"

She licked her lips, watching her oldest son as he

stood up, his straight hair falling down across his forehead, his left hand automatically at the scarf of his Youth uniform, the sleeves of his khaki shirt rolled up as he was wont to do when he ate, but rolled with perfect neatness, perfect order. "I, ahh — promised to meet Frau Heider and we must shop — I don't like to keep her waiting." She watched her son's smile return. "It is good that a school holiday has been declared while your father and the others are away — it is comforting to have your strength during these days, Manfred."

"Thank you, Mother." Manfred smiled, spearing a piece of knockwurst with his fork.

She pushed her chair away from the table and Manfred stood again, out of deference to her, she knew. "You sit and eat your food before it gets cold — there is ice cream in the refrigerator — Manfred, would you see to it that the boys have enough but not too much."

"Of course, Mother." She was already walking across the room, taking up her shawl and her handbag from the small table in the hallway and opening the purse to make sure that she had her key and her money — she had both.

She turned, Manfred, visible in the dining area, still standing, still watching after her. She smiled and blew him a kiss, calling back, "You boys do as your brother Manfred says — especially you, Willy." She let herself out and into the corridor.

As the door closed, she sagged back against the wall — she realized she was sweating.

Helene Sturm told herself it was the pregnancy. She opened her purse, searching it for a handkerchief, clutching the bag against her swollen abdomen as she

143

walked the corridor toward the elevator, mopping her forehead and her throat with the handkerchief, then pushing the elevator call button.

Ten seconds later, the elevator was there and the doors opened. She stepped inside, pushing the mall level button and clamping her right hand, still clutching the handkerchief, on the rail. She watched through the glass back of the elevator tube as the car passed downward so rapidly that, when she was pregnant at least, it almost invariably made her nauseous. But when she was pregnant many things made her nauseous. The car stopped, having descended fourteen floors, and she turned away from the mall level lobby and walked through the doors, putting her handkerchief away in her handbag, walking across the lobby, nodding and smiling as she saw Frau Doster laden with her books.

Helene Sturm reached the doorway to the mall and passed through, the photoelectric eyes opening and closing the door for her.

And she was on the mall. Helene Sturm looked to right and left, then took her shawl and threw it across her shoulders, walking to her right. She passed the glass panel on the side of the company grade officers' quarters building, looking at her slightly distorted reflection. She shifted the shawl slightly where it had upturned the corner of the big white sailor collar, smoothing the maternity top slightly and walking on.

She reached the crossing area and waited, the traffic signals droning "*Vorsicht! Vorsicht!*" then the light shifting from amber to green. She started across the street, looking down at her feet a moment as she picked her way — she felt short in low-heeled shoes but

144

when she was pregnant wearing higher heels hurt her back. Automatically, as she looked up, she splayed her fingers along the seam of her skirt—the baby was kicking again and she did not feel it was seemly to massage her abdomen while walking down a public thoroughfare.

On the opposite side of the street now, she kept walking, a fleeting wave from a passing electric tram car—Frau Dr. Morgensturn, her dentist. Helene Sturm waved back, not thinking Frau Doctor Morgensturn had seen her return the wave because the light had changed and traffic had begun moving again.

As she walked along the mall, the posters were everywhere, the Swastika, the proclamations of glorious victory. She felt her lips downturn slightly—and she felt slightly guilty. She was a direct descendent of one of the most decorated men in the SS. She kept walking, turning the corner into the shopping mall itself, walking on toward the mall side entrance to the market, seeing Anna Heider waiting for her. "I'm sorry I'm late, Anna," she called smiling. Anna Heider's eyes were nervous looking. "I am sorry."

"I thought something had—well, with Manfred and all—"

"No—is Eva inside already?"

"No—she hasn't—wait—" Anna Heider's blue eyes set.

Helene Sturm looked over her shoulder, behind her—Eva Mann was running up on her high heels, the heels clicking on the pavement. Helene Sturm felt herself smiling—she remembered when, five pregnancies ago, she had worn dresses that small and that short.

145

"Eva." Helene Sturm embraced the younger woman.

"Helene—Anna—let us shop." Eva started inside, Helene falling in step after her.

They each took up one of the small computer terminals and one of the styluses and started down the first aisle. "Oh," Anna Heider exclaimed. "My husband hates cottage cheese—now is my chance." Helene watched as Anna's eyes drifted from the displayed container of cottage cheese to the computer terminal in her left hand, her right hand working the stylus to punch the code numbers. They walked on.

In the breakfast food aisle, Eva Mann stopped, studying the representative packages and, for the first time since entering the store, saying anything. "My husband has very painstakingly rearranged unit assignments, and he feels that the Third Corps is at least ninety percent reliable—that other ten percent can be dealt with."

Helene Sturm licked her lips—she had forgotten to wear lipstick and she set down her terminal and her stylus and started searching her handbag for it. "When, then?"

"Whatever befalls," Eva Mann said, marking her terminal with her stylus. "The Third Corps will return here for the Unity Day celebration—that is when—" She fell silent, then raised her voice, "That is when I told my husband that since he is almost never home for breakfast with the children, he should let the children determine their own preference in breakfast cereal—his mother always made him eat hot oatmeal."

Helene Sturm nodded, not knowing what else to do. Anna Heider whispered hoarsely, "They're gone."

Helene Sturm glanced once furtively over her left shoulder—the three women, wives of party officials, had continued down the aisle. Eva was talking again. "On Unity Day—that is when The Leader will be assassinated and the Third Corps will assault the SS contingent still here. Once that happens, the First and Second Corps and the Condor Squadron will return and declare martial law and the real battle will begin. But with The Leader gone and the SS neutralized here, at least we'll have a chance of holding the Complex and drying up their supplies."

Helene noticed Eva Mann was looking at her strangely. "You worry for Helmut and your brother Sigfried."

"Helmut will hate me—Sigfried will hate me. Manfred will hate me, too, I think."

"Helmut is a Nazi, but he is reasonable—he loves you, he loves you and the children," Eva told her, smiling.

They began to walk again, Helene looking up to determine which was the better buy—the 340 gram box of pancake mix or the 510 gram box. As she looked up, she could see the calendar, part of the diode timepiece over the checkout counters. Not much time remained at all until the thirtieth of January and she was very afraid. But a sense of what was right and what was wrong had been something she could not deny ever since she was a little girl.

She decided on the larger box of pancake mix. And perhaps her oldest son Manfred would be lost to her, but Willy and her other two sons, and the life in her womb—they would all know freedom.

Helene Sturm started again along the aisle.

147

Chapter Forty

There was a slight overhang of rock and she watched the rain, which had begun, she estimated, an hour earlier. Rain dripped now from the rock overhang—Natalia Anastasia Tiemerovna, naked, wrists and ankles bound to spikes driven into the living rock, her body spread-eagled, her body weight sagging from the ropes which bound her wrists, was past shivering. She had awakened this way, having no idea how long she had been unconscious, a burning pain in her back and at the base of her skull.

Being with John Rourke had taught her to never abandon hope—and she had at least been close enough to kill her husband, but chance had interceded and one of his guards intervened before she was able to accomplish the task. But she was still close to Vladmir Karamatsov and knew him well enough that she would be even closer—the question was to have the freedom of action necessary to kill while she still possessed the strength and will. The desire, she realized, would only grow.

She heard footsteps along the rocks and turned her head to the right, her neck aching her.

It was Karamatsov.

"You are awake—excellent. I came to tell you what it will be that you must first endure—so you will reap the full benefit of it both mentally and physically. I

148

shall return in two hours. Before I mate with you again, after all these years, you must be purified of this American Rourke, of his taint —"

"He and I have never —"

"Yes — you said that before. But I must be sure. In order to purify you, I have chosen a faultless method. A hot iron — to burn away all that is foul within you. I think you should find the effect interesting — I have utilized such a device before, on women from the Wild Tribes of Europe. But they were very much like animals, and so the full extent of the reaction was difficult to judge."

"You are insane, Vladmir — let the others go. You can do with me what you want, then."

He laughed. "I can do with you what I want now — the others — no. You still have that to look forward to as well, watching as Rourke's wife and daughter and the other girl and the black woman are raped, beaten. Powerless to help them — that too should be an interesting effect. Now — you should genuinely enjoy this next part." She watched as he reached under his black leather jacket, producing a small leatherette case — it was a syringe kit, she knew. "Curious that some good can arise from adversity. A plant I had never known of before — it may be some hybrid as a result of the radiation after the Night of The War, or perhaps due to the rigors of the nearly airless climate. It appears to be some sort of mushroom. But you know science was never one of my areas of interest. But it has the most marvelous effects." She watched — feeling sweat on her upper lip — despite the cold — as he withdrew a syringe from the leatherette case. "Only a modest amount seems to induce some sort of condition very similar to paranoid schizophrenia. The total inability to concentrate, all consuming fear—hallucinations. And it leaves the subject afterward physically exhausted." He smiled, gesturing expansively with the hypodermic as he brought it closer to her. "It also works as a muscle relaxant. I noticed your neck seemed stiff—this will fix that. But it's rather strong muscle relaxant, I'm afraid. You will lose all control of bodily functions. I'm afraid it will make quite a mess—on you and on the rocks. But we can clean you up enough to use the hot iron. And this outdoor location—I was about to apologize for it—but at least you won't have to bother yourself about dirtying a floor. And the various smells should dissipate more rapidly."

"I hate you," she whispered.

"Ahh—music to my ears. And just think." She felt the hypodermic prick at the skin of her interior left forearm. "If you hate me now—just think how you'll feel in a little while." She tried moving her arm, but he pinned it against the rock as he stabbed the needle into her flesh.

He stepped back. She watched him—watched him laughing at her as the sick feeling spread into her stomach and her body lurched as she lost total control of her bowels.

Chapter Forty-One

He reached out his left hand, impacting hard against the face of the black-clad Soviet guard, smashing the head rearward, against the jagged rock face, a crunching sound, the body slumping downward.

John Rourke bent over him, taking up the assault rifle, removing the magazine. He had taught himself how to disassemble the new Soviet weapon. He worked the pin which allowed the action to break open for cleaning, then withdrew the bolt.

He dropped the useless rifle to the rocks, then threw the bolt up into the rocks from which he had come. Stealth and silence were useful, but not his overriding concern. Speed was his overriding concern.

The truck was parked more than a mile away. This was the first of the Soviet guards he had encountered.

Picking up his own rifle, John Rourke moved ahead, along the rocks, his musette bag bulging with spare magazines, the rucksack he had taken bulging with the guns of the people he intended to save at whatever cost from Vladmir Karamatsov. Across his back were two assault rifles beyond the M-16 he already carried in his hand. He didn't contemplate the added weight he carried. It had slowed his climb into the rocks, and slowed him now as he picked his way forward.

But necessity was a more demanding mistress than

convenience ever could be.

Sarah. Annie. Madison. Dr. Halverson. Lieutenant Kurinami.

"Natalia," he whispered.

He would get her back and all of them with her.

Soon — soon there would be another guard to kill.

"One less to kill later," John Rourke rasped under his breath as he moved on.

Chapter Forty-Two

Her lips were cut and bleeding from contact with the ropes that had bound Akiro Kurinami's hands to the spike, but as she sagged forward onto her chest, she smiled—Kurinami was at work on the knots securing the ropes to her ankles. And her hands were free.

"I have them," he almost hissed.

Sarah Rourke rolled over onto her back, not yet trusting her legs to move. She nodded. "Get Dr. Halverson free—I'll work on Madison after I see how Annie is." Sarah Rourke crawled on knees and elbows across the ground to the far side of the tent—her daughter was breathing more regularly and seemed to be coming around. Sarah didn't undo the gag lest Annie make some loud sound upon awakening.

She turned to Madison—her defacto daughter-in-law. "Michael'll be all right—don't worry. He's just like his father—that's his only problem—I'll have you out of these in a few seconds." She released the gag from Madison's mouth, the girl's head sagging forward, her breathing heavy.

"I should have done more—"

"You tried," Sarah told her, breaking still more nails working to undo the ropes. "And you'll have plenty of chance to, once we get out of here if—"

There was a scream. A woman's scream, but almost inhuman sounding.

It could only be one person —

Sarah Rourke worked frantically at the ropes now, Madison's hands free, the girl rubbing her wrists. "I can get my own ankles."

"Good girl." Sarah turned, on her blue-jeaned knees still, to her daughter, Annie opening her eyes. Sarah reached to Annie's face and undid the gag at the nape of her neck. "Annie — don't make any noise — are you all right?"

"What —"

"Kurinami got himself free enough that I could untie his wrists — we're on our way."

"I'm gonna get that bastard that hit me." Annie coughed.

"Who taught you to talk like that — your father? A girl your age shouldn't —" But she suddenly remembered her daughter was nearly her own age.

The scream came again — a scream more terrifying than anything Sarah had ever heard, in labor rooms when she had worked at a hospital before she had married John Rourke, in the camps among the wounded and the dying after the Night of The War.

A scream that was beyond agony.

Annie's brown eyes opened wide and looked up at her as Sarah worked to untie her daughter's wrists.

"It's Natalia," Sarah said evenly, calmly. "Looks like we've gotta get her out of here, too."

Chapter Forty-Three

Michael's pulse rate was lowering. "Shit," Paul Rubenstein snarled. He picked up the radio microphone, checking the storage battery connections. "Paul Rubenstein to Eden One — Ground to Eden One — over."

There was static only for a moment, then a voice. "This is Jeff Styles — I'm science officer — hang on a minute, Mr. Rubenstein — I'll get Captain Dodd — over."

Rubenstein depressed the push-to-talk button quickly. "Get him damn fast. I've got most the runway cleared — at least one shuttle has to land pronto. I've got a man dying down here — he needs medical care and he needs blood — I mean, real fast. Over."

"I'm gettin' him, sir — hang on — Styles over."

Raul Rubenstein stood up, pacing the tent floor, waiting for Dodd to come back over the radio.

Less than a mile of the sand needed to be cleared — and only one pylon was left from the second bridge. The sand wasn't very much and there wasn't very much of the pylon either.

If he could get at least one of the ships down in time, Michael could be saved — he felt it inside of him.

A crackle of static, then a voice over the radio. "Dodd to Mr. Rubenstein. Eden One to Ground — come in, Mr. Rubenstein. Over."

Rubenstein had the microphone in his right fist.

"This is Rubenstein—I've gotta get at least one of you guys down here in the next couple of hours. John Rourke has gone off to rescue the rest of his family and Kurinami and Halverson from the Russians. Michael's pulse is weakening and his blood pressure is way down—John taught me how to check it. He needs a doctor and he needs blood—fast or we'll lose him." He cleared his throat. "Rubenstein over."

Dodd's voice—"Mr. Rubenstein—Jeff Styles appraised me of the runway conditions you mentioned—all clear? Over."

"Almost—two hours' work at the top and you'll have the smoothest runway you ever saw. Over."

"Then we'll be seeing you—I understand the urgency of your situation. I understand also I may have an attack force of Soviet gunships to contend with when I bring her in. Over."

Rubenstein depressed the push-to-talk button. "I've got assault rifles down here. The gunship, Dr. Rourke left behind—I can fiddle with the mounts for the machine guns and use them against any of the gunships—or at least try. If you don't come down, the son of a man who risked his life and his family's lives to make a landing strip for you is gonna die. And I wouldn't want John Rourke mad at me. Over."

"Mr. Rubenstein—if your Dr. Rourke is off fighting the Soviets, it seems he's doing a job we sort of missed out on last time—all of us. Well—we won't miss out on it this time. I'm the only pilot of the six primary shuttle pilots with combat experience. And I know how to fly choppers—I did that for a while in Viet Nam under circumstances so peculiar even a five-hundred-year-old man like you wouldn't believe them.

Eden One is coming down and if we make it, we'll secure the area and get the rest of the fleet down double quick. I'll begin de-orbiting procedure in roughly two hours. I should be on the ground in less than three. Oh — and that other airborne force we've detected — it appears to be comprised of gunships as well. It should be coming your way — it's airborne again out of Alabama. Dodd over — oh — good luck."

"Thanks — out."

"Eden One out." Dodd's voice was replaced by static now.

Paul Rubenstein set down the microphone and checked Michael — Michael was feverish which could mean infection had crept into one of the wounds.

Paul Rubenstein started through the tent flap, running, running toward the earth mover so he could complete work on the runway surface.

The mounts for the helicopter's machine guns.

Getting ready — there was a lot to do. Paul Rubenstein ran harder.

Chapter Forty-Four

The thing that was crawling across her left breast was watching her. It was some kind of snake except that it had more legs than she could count and small horns on each side of the head and its eyes were red, but the face was Vladmir's face and she knew that she was screaming, and she tried telling herself that none of it was real. But the screaming was real, wasn't it?

The screaming had to be real and she could feel the countless tiny feet at the ends of the countless tiny legs as the creature moved across her flesh and she shrieked at it to stop, finally calling it by name— "Vladmir!"

There was another creature—on her right breast and sometimes its face looked like John Rourke's face, but then it would snap at the creature with Vladmir's face and then suddenly it, too, would have Vladmir's face and then the creature would disappear and then the first creature was gone and she looked down toward the rocks beneath her—snakes and roaches crawled along the rocks and out of the mire between her legs there on the rocks the creature was coming again—it crawled from the ooze, Vladmir's face laughing as the creature started up the inside of her right calf and she screamed.

All the snakes on the ground were watching her—they were laughing at her. The roaches were piling on top of one another, like they were forming a living chain, but the chain was now more like a ladder and the top one on the pile was crawling onto her bare foot and she screamed again.

The creature with Vladmir's face was on the side of her right thigh now, and she could hear his laughter, feel the slime of the wet body as it slithered against her flesh. "Help me!"

The thing was coming closer to her and she could feel its horned head prodding her and creeping into her—it wanted to mate with her, and she screamed again and she couldn't breathe and her throat was very tight—the thing was disappearing inside her and she could hear the laughter from inside herself now as the roaches crawled along their living chain and wormed up her right leg—would they follow the other thing inside of her?

And she could see inside herself, and the horns on the head of the creature glowed orange with heat and the flame was consuming her insides, and she screamed as the creature moved within her and shrieked with laughter, and Natalia screamed and screamed and screamed and screamed.

Chapter Forty-Five

Kurinami to her left, Annie to her right, Sarah Rourke glanced behind her once at Madison and Elaine Halverson. Sarah edged back the tent flap, peering outside — again the screaming and at the far side of the encampment, Sarah Rourke could see her — even in agony, there was a certain beauty about Natalia, "The Russian Woman." She appeared naked, her body twisting and contorting as she screamed, some of the personnel of the compound openly staring at her, others trying to ignore her, it seemed.

Sarah Rourke looked away from Natalia. To the left of the tent, toward the center of the camp and toward the improvised airfield where the helicopters were parked, stood two men, assault rifles slung lazily crossbody, across their backs. These were her guards, she realized.

She let the tent flap drop back in place slowly, then turned to whisper to the others. "Two men near us — each one of them is carrying one of those funny-looking assault rifles, and each one of them has a flap holster with a pistol in it. That's four weapons and there are five of us. Kurinami is a weapon — but each one of them has a bayonet — "

"Ahh — I faithfully practiced a kata involving machetes — this would be much similar."

Sarah Rourke looked at the Japanese and smiled.

Then she looked at Madison. "Those lessons Michael was giving you—can you handle a rifle, do you think?"

"Yes, Mother Rourke—I want to hurt these men; I can use a rifle."

Sarah smiled. "Good girl. Then a rifle for you, a rifle for me—Annie, you take a pistol, and Elaine—you take a pistol as well."

"I don't know much about guns—if it doesn't work like a Colt—"

"I'll fix it to work for you," Annie told the woman.

"Fine—now." Sarah looked at Madison. "At the count of three, I want you to shout for help—not too loudly— I only want those two guards to hear you, not the whole camp. Kurinami and I'll be ready, Annie and Dr. Halverson will back us up." Sarah Rourke picked up the spike Kurinami had twisted out of the rocky ground—she hefted it in her right hand, ready.

"All right—I'm counting to three—be ready." Sarah Rourke raised her left thumb. "One." Then the forefinger. "Two." Then, after a second's pause, her middle finger. "Three."

Madison didn't shriek—it was more like a cry for assistance, just what it should be, Sarah thought. "Help me—oh, please—my God—help me!"

Sarah felt herself smile—the girl would make a good Rourke.

Sarah stepped back, the spike raised in her right fist, held like a dagger, Kurinami beside her.

The tent flap opened, a face peering inside. "Akiro," Sarah hissed, and Kurinami's hands flashed forward and the man's body was jerked inside, Kurinami pinning the man, in the fleeting second

161

while Sarah awaited her own target, Sarah watching as his right fist hammered downward into the Adam's apple of the already supine and very terrified-looking Russian boy.

Sarah saw the movement—the second guard, his rifle coming in first—Sarah's right arm arced downward, the spike driving into the man's right forearm, blood spurting upward, the man's body already half through the tent flap, Sarah's right hand going for his face, like she had seen it done so many times, the heel of the hand, her forearm straight, hammering upward against the base of the nose. His eyes registered surprise. The nose crunched upward, blood spraying from it, Sarah involuntarily turning her eyes away, the man's body collapsing as Kurinami's hands flashed forward, Kurinami's right hand killing the man an unnecessary second time, the right hand impacting the windpipe, the body impacting the ground.

Sarah wheeled half right—Elaine Halverson had the first dead guard's pistol, and Annie tossed the dead man's rifle and then his utility belt with the spare magazines it contained.

Sarah looped the belt over her left shoulder, working what appeared to be the rifle's bolt handle, finding the safety/selector, moving it to what she hoped was full auto. "Anybody speak Russian?"

"I do—a little." Kurinami smiled.

"This mean pull the trigger and bang?" She showed him the receiver.

Kurinami laughed. "Indeed it does, I think."

Sarah nodded. Kurinami had both bayonets now, Annie the other pistol and Madison—quiet, beautiful, probably pregnant Madison—the other assault rifle, the utility belt that went with it worn from her left shoulder to her right side.

"Ready? We go up the middle, to free Natalia — we don't leave without her," Sarah Rourke told them. "Then we fight our way back toward one of the helicopters and Lieutenant Kurinami flies us out of here — we hope." Then Sarah leaned toward Annie, kissing her as she embraced her. "I love you — so much." She placed her arms around Madison. "My daughter, too — and the child in you — I love you both." Then Sarah turned toward the tent flap. "Did somebody help Elaine with her pistol?"

"I did, Momma," Annie's voice came back.

"Let's kill those bastards," Sarah Rourke almost whispered, pushing through the tent flap, ready to die for a woman she should have hated.

Chapter Forty-Six

Natalia felt her body tremble—but the horrible fantasies were gone. But what she saw before her was worse—Vladmir Karamatsov, a bayonet in his left fist, the third of the blade from the point back yellow-orange and smoking with heat, a fire on the ground beside him, another of the bayonets there, already beginning to glow.

"Cauterizing a wound, my dear," Karamatsov whispered to her, cooed to her, smiling.

She felt ashamed of the filth between her legs, of her smell, and she felt this more than fear. And more than this, she felt shame for having failed to kill Karamatsov, for having failed to rescue Sarah and Annie and Madison and Dr. Halverson and Lieutenant Kurinami.

She looked her husband in the eyes, her voice surprising her with its steadiness. "If there is a life after death, I'll come back to destroy your dreams, to twist your mind more than it is already twisted—to kill you if I can."

Karamatsov laughed, the glowing bayonet extending toward her loins. "But I'm afraid, darling, that death will not come to you for quite a long time and so if you can come back to haunt me, you won't have your chance for the longest, most delicious time." She could feel the heat radiating from the knife blade, her mouth open to scream a curse at him before she could only scream in pain; her eyes drifted from his eyes to the knife as it moved toward her millimeter by millimeter, the tip of it against the hair there, some of the hair starting to smolder as she sucked in her breath and drew herself back against the rock face, its coldness chilling her—the fear gnawing at her. "I have a tape recorder going, so I can remember this moment forever." He moved the knife forward.

Natalia closed her eyes and shouted, "Rot in hell!" She could feel the heat. . . .

John Rourke had the Python in both fists—he didn't trust the M-16 to be that accurate. To kill would be easier, but the knife could still plunge forward—to disable the arm was the only way. His finger moved against the trigger of the Metalifed and Mag-Na-Ported Colt, the hammer to full stand. The pistol bucked lightly once in his hands and the scream that had begun in Natalia's throat, the scream he had heard, felt in his insides, died. Vladmir Karamatsov shrieked, "No!" The glowing bayonet sprang upward from his left arm, Karamatsov's right hand clamping over his left forearm as Rourke threw himself into a run, the distance between him and the man he so wanted to kill again less than fifty yards, the bayonet clattering to the rocks, rain pouring down in sheets as Rourke double actioned the Python, gut shooting the guard who had been standing beside Karamatsov, the man's assault rifle rising to fire. Rourke swung the muzzle toward Karamatsov, firing, Karamatsov seeming to stumble on the rocks, skidding, recovering, running, gunfire suddenly all around Rourke as he ran—twenty-five yards now.

Rourke swung the muzzle of the Python right—

"Sarah!" His wife, an assault rifle blazing from her hands, was running from the far end of the camp, Annie with her, Madison half walking behind them, firing an assault rifle behind her, Dr. Halverson firing a pistol point-blank into the face of an attacker, the Japanese, Kurinami, a knife in each hand, hacking, slashing, killing his way forward.

Sarah's assault rifle spit death, the waves of Soviet forces around her going down or running to cover as Rourke looked back toward Natalia, running — a single shout echoed over the tumult — Natalia's voice: "I love you!"

Chapter Forty-Seven

Karamatsov had vanished into the tumult as Rourke emptied the Python into the torso of a man armed with an assault rifle who was about to shoot Natalia. The KGB man's body lurched away from her. Rourke was beside her now, stuffing the Python into the leather, grabbing the big Gerber from his belt. "Watch behind me, Natalia." He hacked the blade against the ropes binding her left ankle. He hacked with the blade again, the ropes, already frayed from the first bite of the blade, snapping. Natalia's body visibly sagged as Rourke worked the knife against the ropes binding the right ankle.

Her body weight slumped downward even more, Rourke rising, glancing behind him once, Sarah and the others closing toward his position, Rourke taking the MkII and sawing the ropes free of Natalia's left wrist. "Lean on me." He felt her left arm rest across his right shoulder, limply.

The right wrist — he had her free and her body fell against him. "I'm too dirty," she gasped — Rourke swept her up into his arms, naked, holding her against him. Close. He moved her away from the wet rocks to which she had been bound, setting her down on the ground for an instant, sheathing the spear-pointed Gerber. Rourke slipped the rucksack straps and the slings for the M-16 rifles, stripping away his battered brown leather bomber jacket then, easing Natalia up into a sitting position, putting the jacket around her trembling shoulders. "I — I tried," she gasped. "I almost had him — but someone struck me down from behind and I woke up —"

"Worry about it later — we gotta get out of here — slip your arms into the jacket —"

"I'm filthy — I'll —"

"Do as you're told —"

"I can still shoot — give me a gun —"

"Better than that." Rourke shoved the rucksack toward her as she leaned back on one elbow. Sarah and Annie and the others were holding back the Russians for the moment, and Rourke reached into the musette bag slung at his left side — his syringe kit. He had seen the mark on the inside of Natalia's left forearm and he pulled her left arm toward him, swabbing the area from the previous injection with a pre-soaked alcohol-saturated cotton ball.

He started to bring the point of one of the hypos toward her arm — and involuntarily it seemed, Natalia drew her arm back. "Tetanus shot — then I've got a B-complex for you to keep going —"

"Vladmir — he gave me some type of hallucinogen — it — it — it made me see these horrible things, feel them — crawling up inside of me and —"

Rourke looked into her almost surreal blue eyes — they were clearer seeming than when he had cut her down a moment earlier. "I'm going to kill him — he's a walking dead man." Rourke gave her the first shot, swabbing an area further up her arm, finding a vein and administering a second shot — he bent her arm back at the elbow, his jacket's sleeve pushed above it.

Pocketing the syringe kit in the musette bag, Rourke drew one of the M-16s from the ground beside him, working the bolt, setting the selector at full auto, on his knees beside Natalia still, spraying the M-16 to-ward a knot of Soviet troopers. And then Sarah was beside him. As Rourke started to change sticks in the M-16, Sarah half shouted, "Michael—how is—"

"Alive—but he needs a transfusion—from you or from Annie—I gave him two pints—he's holding on—Paul's looking after him—with all of you here I had to come—"

"I understand," Sarah interrupted. "Kurinami was going to fly us out of here after we got to Natalia—why don't you fly one chopper now, Kurinami the other—"

Natalia's voice sounded as Rourke slapped the fresh magazine home. "I don't think I could walk far—but I can fly one of those new helicopters—it doesn't re-quire using your legs."

Annie was on Rourke's other side now, one of the Stechkin type pistols blazing from her right fist. "Daddy—turn your eyes the other way—"

Rourke looked to his left, staring at her—"What the hell do you—"

"I'm giving Natalia my slip to cover her—look away." Rourke stabbed the M-16 toward more of the Soviet troopers, firing. He saw a flash of white pass-ing from his left side and reappearing on his right. "Help her, Momma."

"Ease yourself up—let me get this up along your legs—lean on me—damn it—lean on me."

Rourke didn't look at his wife and Natalia—he looked at his daughter—she was pulling her skirt down over her legs. "What the hell happened to your face?"

"A rifle butt — I saw the son of a bitch that did it — "

"Don't talk like that — who the hell taught you that kind of language?"

"I saw him when we left the tent and I shot him in the face and he's dead — I'm fine. And I'll talk the way I want — I'm almost twenty-eight years old, remember?"

"Yeah — well" — Rourke fired the M-16 again, peeling two men away from Kurinami as the Japanese hacked and slashed with his bayonets.

"Let's get the hell out of here," Rourke rasped, to his feet, ramming a fresh magazine in his M-16. "Annie — take that rucksack and distribute the weapons — "

"I'll help Natalia get where we're going," Sarah half shouted from beside him. Rourke turned to look at the two women, the two women he loved. Natalia looked slightly ridiculous, the brown leather jacket zipped in front and miles too big for her, Annie's slip covering her legs, the double holster rig around her waist, her face drawn, pained. Sarah, wearing her inevitable blue jeans and a faded blue T-shirt, a bandana tied around her hair, was struggling to get Natalia from her knees to a standing position. Both of them looked like beautiful drowned rats.

"I'll help, too," Annie snapped. "You distribute the weapons!" Rourke's daughter thrust the rucksack into his left hand. She had the belt for the Scoremaster around her waist and Sarah held the Trapper Scorpion .45 in her left fist, Natalia sagged against her, standing, Natalia's left arm draped across Sarah's shoulders. In Natalia's right fist was one of the L-Frames.

Rourke shook his head. "Women—shit." He grabbed up the other two M-16s now, starting ahead, firing out the M-16 in his right hand, tossing Elaine Halverson the rucksack. "Your pistol and Kurinami's pistol—some spare magazines—hold onto them."

Rourke dropped the emptied M-16 down on its sling, a fresh M-16 in each fist now as he started ahead, the three women just behind him as he looked back once, Elaine Halverson and Kurinami bringing up the rear, Kurinami now with a pistol in his right fist, a bayonet in his left. "Where the hell is Madison?"

"I don't know," Sarah shouted back.

But then Rourke saw her—to the far side of the camp, one of the Soviet assault rifles in her hands, spraying it into a concentration of Soviet troops. "Damn girl's gonna get herself killed and my grandson, too!"

"What if it's a granddaughter?" Sarah shouted from behind him, but Rourke was already running toward Madison—her assault rifle had stopped firing. The rain was falling more heavily now, coming in sheets as the wind picked up, Rourke feeling the tiredness, the fatigue as he ran, still exhausted from the previous night's work and worn down by the transfusions he had given Michael. If Sarah and Natalia and Annie and Madison had not been in danger, if necessity hadn't required that he be capable of flying the helicopter to knock out the bridge supports, he would have given his son all his blood gladly and died to save him.

John Rourke forced himself to keep moving, Madison gamely if ineffectively hammering at one of the

Soviet troopers with the butt of the Russian assault rifle, losing it, the man wrestling her down as Rourke reached the fringe of the group around her.

A three-round burst into the small of the back of one of them and the man went down, both M-16s firing now as some of the Soviet personnel turned toward him, Rourke cutting them down.

Both M-16s were empty, Rourke letting the Colt assault rifles drop to his sides, his left fist clipping the jaw of one man, the heel of his right hand impacting another man's face at the base of the nose, breaking the nose, driving the bone upward to puncture the ethmoid bone and pierce the brain.

The twin Detonics Scoremaster pistols he had taken from The Place—in his hands now, the hammers already back, his right and left thumb working down the ambidextrous safeties, the pistols barking from each hand as his fists tightened on them. His first fingers worked the triggers and two more of the Soviet personnel went down, 185-grain JHPs thudding into them.

Rourke kept moving, a Soviet trooper crashing the butt of a rifle down toward the kneeling Madison, her blond hair soaked, plastered across her forehead as the wind tore at her skirt, her arms raised in self-defense, a look of defiance—Rourke was proud of his "daughter-in-law"—etched across her face, her blue eyes wide.

Rourke fired both Scoremasters simultaneously, killing the man in his tracks.

The body crumpled, Madison edging away, Rourke beside her now, shifting one of the M-16s from his body, handing it to her as he kept firing into the Soviet

172

forces with the Scoremasters. "Spare magazines in the musette bag—"

"What's—what's a musette—"

"It looks like a canvas purse—this thing." Rourke emptied the pistol in his right hand, then the pistol in his left. "Here—reload these, too." Rourke set the pistols on the wet rocks beside her knees.

"All right." He glanced at her as she began fumbling in the bag.

Rourke's hands moved to the double Alessi rig under his armpits, first the pistol under the left arm, then the one under the right breaking through the trigger guard snap closures, his thumbs jacking back the hammers of the twin Detonics .45s.

He stabbed both pistols forward, firing both into the chest of one of the Soviet troopers charging toward them, one of the new Soviet assault rifles blazing. The man went down.

Rourke was standing now, Madison kneeling beside him, both pistols emptying into a knot of Soviet troopers rushing them. Rourke worked down the slide stops and jammed the pistols into his belt, starting to reach for one of the empty M-16s to reload it. He would be too late, he realized, starting to hurtle himself toward Madison, to protect her with his body as two Soviet troopers charged. But there was a burst of assault rifle fire from beside him—Madison, an M-16 in her tiny fists—both troopers were down.

"Your pistols," she half shrieked, handing the Scoremasters up to him.

Rourke took them, working the slide stops to chamber the first rounds, then shouting to the girl beside him, "Come on, sweetheart—stay with me." Rourke started forward, Madison at his left side, the rain, almost impossibly, heavier now, huge drops pelting at his face, his glasses streaming with it, his clothes soaked and sticking to his body.

"Yes, Father Rourke," he heard the girl saying.

He glanced to her once and laughed. "Yes, Daughter Rourke." He fired the twin Detonics Scoremasters, cutting down still another of the Soviet troopers. But the enemy was dispersing now toward the helicopters, not running from him, but not from Sarah and the others either. He looked overhead—black gunships filled the rain drenched grey sky—emblazoned on their fuselages was a symbol he thought he would never see again—a black Swastika, outlined in white.

Chapter Forty-Eight

Wolfgang Mann looked at his rank insignia — he resented it. He was a colonel in the Wermacht, but his rank was SS, standarten führer. "Attack the Soviet personnel on the ground and in the air — those others fighting there, without uniforms — if they can successfully be captured, do so, but they are not to be harmed — not yet." He turned his attention from the teardrop-shaped microphone near his mouth to the controls of the helicopter, banking now, leveling off, coming in for the first attack run against the Communists. Speaking into the microphone he said, "Follow me." Then he armed his missiles. "Fire at targets of opportunity — remember my admonition against harming the non-Soviet personnel." Mann depressed the fire control button for his starboard missiles, discharging the primary tube. The contrail then one of the Soviet choppers just starting airborne vaporized in a ball of flame.

The windshield wipers were maddening as he stared through his rain-streaming windscreen. "This is Mann — do it just like that." He started going for altitude as the rest of the Condor Squadron followed in on the targets.

If there were other humans alive, humans not aligned with the Soviets — he had anticipated this helicopter force would be Soviet — then reason dictated these were Americans, Americans with their classic lust for freedom.

He could use such persons with such desires — to help in his own cause. The troop ships were on the horizon and Mann switched frequencies on the radio, ordering his copilot: "Take over the controls on three — one, two — they are yours — three." He spoke into his microphone as the helicopter lurched once, then continued to climb over the field of battle. "This is Standarten Führer Wolfgang Mann — Third Corps will stay in reserve — First and Second Corps, to the ground. There appear to be several women and two men who are fighting against the Soviet force. They are not to be harmed but taken prisoner if possible for my personal interrogation. I repeat — under no circumstances are they to be harmed. First and Second Corps move out." He glanced to his copilot. "I'll take it again — release control to me, now!" And he had the yoke, banking the chopper and dropping in altitude to skim over the field — the possible Americans, whoever they were, seemed to be consolidating their position near three helicopters at the far edge of the encampment. Mann flew over them, one of the women — she looked ridiculous, a leather jacket and a white slip all that she wore, firing a pistol toward him. A smile crossed his lips — whoever they were, they could fight. He could use that talent as well.

Chapter Forty-Nine

Kurinami already had one of the Soviet machines airborne, Elaine Halverson and Annie with him. As Rourke shoved Madison in through the open fuselage door of a second helicopter, he could see Natalia positioning herself in the cockpit of a third, Sarah framed in the open fuselage doorway, firing a Soviet assault rifle.

Rourke snapped to Madison — "Keep low, put down some fire to keep 'em away as we try and get off the ground." Rourke started firing the controls, wishing the temperature and pressure levels to rise, pushing open a storm vent beside the pilot's seat, ramming his left fist through it, firing one of the Scoremasters toward the Soviet troops racing past them.

He had lost Vladmir Karamatsov — he knew that. But he also knew where Karamatsov would go — final revenge. Karamatsov would take whatever force he could spare from fighting the superior Nazi forces and go toward the camp, to kill Michael, to kill Paul, to taste the revenge Rourke had denied him, however little, however much more Karamatsov craved it.

Rourke adjusted the mixture, the main rotor's RPMs nearly to a satisfactory level. Natalia's machine was getting airborne, Sarah crouched in the doorframe now, still firing into the Soviets.

"Hang on, Madison — we gotta boogie, sweetheart."

Rourke started flipping switches—it was time to be airborne, the RPM level nearly sufficient, the temperatures nearly high enough.

Rourke activated his attack computer, overriding the computerized targeting so he could operate fire control manually. He could feel the machine beginning to rise. The Nazi gunships were not firing toward Natalia's or Kurinami's craft. Rourke wondered why, but he, too, withheld fire from the Nazis, seeking one of the Soviet choppers as a target.

He had one as they were airborne and Rourke fired one of the portside missiles. The machine vaporized, a black and orange fireball hissing skyward, steam rising from the pieces of wreckage as they floated downward in the cold rain.

Rourke shivered, wet, feeling Madison behind him. "A blanket, Father Rourke."

She covered his shoulders with it. Rourke started to tell her to use it, but instead, he looked back at her for a moment and smiled. "Thanks, Madison."

Nazi troop-carrying helicopters were landing now, men spilling from them, sand-colored khakis, assault rifles in their hands, firing, other troop ships still airborne, men rapelling from them, Soviet choppers spraying the lowered ropes with machine gun fire, men falling to their deaths, Nazi helicopters closing in, launching missiles toward the Soviet helicopters.

But in the distance, passing out of sight over the horizon, Rourke could see a squadron of at least eight helicopters—and they were heading southwest—toward the camp, toward Michael.

Rourke spoke into his headset microphone. "Natalia—Kurinami—come back if you hear me. Rourke over."

"I hear you, John—are you all right? Natalia, over."

"This is Kurinami, doctor—you are well?"

"We're fine—those choppers that just went over the horizon—we've gotta intercept them—it'll be Karamatsov and he's heading to the camp to get Michael—break off here. Rourke out!"

"How fast can this air machine fly, Father Rourke?" Madison asked, easing into the copilot's seat beside him.

He looked at his daughter-in-law and smiled. "We're gonna find out, sweetheart—fasten that seat belt." Rourke found one of his thin dark tobacco cigars in his shirt pocket—it was wet but the Zippo still lit it, the smell like burning rope because of the wetness.

As he inhaled the grey smoke deep into his lungs, then exhaled, he throttled out the pirated Soviet gunship.

Perhaps the most important rendezvous of his life awaited him, John Rourke thought.

Chapter Fifty

"Captain Popovski—signal the attack force to make best speed toward the campsite and to hold back five miles off," Karamatsov told the younger man beside him.

"Comrade colonel—perhaps with the enemy force so near—"

Karamatsov looked at Popovski, raising his left eyebrow. "You question my orders, Popovski?"

"No, comrade colonel—I did not mean to imply—"

"Had I killed his son, he would have pursued me throughout the camp after releasing my wife. So his son still lives. That is why Natalia came in his stead. He and the Jew were working to save the boy. We will kill the boy."

Karamatsov heard Popovski mutter something into the headset radio, then Popovski turned to him, Karamatsov looking away, staring at the ground beneath them, seeing the spray of rain water pelted by the rotor blades above them. "What is it?"

"Comrade colonel—a message from the underground city—the Eden Project. One of the six vessels is de-orbiting—wait—there is more." Karamatsov looked at Popovski as the young man concentrated on the radio headset. "Comrade colonel—one of the Eden Project vessels, the one that was making contact with the Rourke encampment in Southern Georgia—it is about to land — within the hour it is estimated — radio transmissions have been monitored an —"

"Good," Karamatsov interrupted. "With our gunships, we shall destroy Eden One as it lands, then kill Rourke's son and Rourke's Jew friend. Then we shall leave the field and rendezvous with our support planes and regroup for a final attack against Rourke and his band."

"But — but, comrade colonel — the Nazis — are they not the greater threat to our —"

"You tread dangerous ground, Popovski," Karamatsov told his subordinate and Karamatsov looked away, studying the pattern of the sheets of rain as they passed the fuselage windows.

If he thought there were a God he would have thought God were crying. And in case there were, he intended to give this God ample reason for tears.

"Order maximum speed to the Rourke campsite — we mustn't miss our appointment, Popovski — not by even a second." He rubbed at his injured left forearm. Something else for which to repay his wife and her lover, John Rourke.

He half heard Popovski issue his orders to the other gunships. But he was thinking of other things.

Chapter Fifty-One

Paul Rubenstein leaned over Michael Rourke, the boy—Paul could not help but think of him that way despite the fact Michael was chronologically older than he was now—barely breathing. "Don't worry, Michael—they'll be on the ground soon and Commander Dodd is your blood type. And the science officer—he thinks he can use the transfusion equipment and give you some of Captain Dodd's blood. You'll live—you gotta live." Paul Rubenstein stood to his full height, suddenly cold, pulling his olive drab field jacket closer about him. "You'll live," he whispered, then bent over the unconscious man to pull the blankets higher across Michael's chest.

Paul Rubenstein turned away and picked up his Schmeisser and walked through the tent flap. The rain made the possibilities for a good landing even more remote, would make the cleared highway surface that much slicker, that much poorer traction for Eden One.

He had shifted the frequency of the Soviet helicopter to the frequency of Eden One. He ran toward the Soviet chopper through the rain now, skipping larger puddles, his head tucked down into his collar as best he could. He had remounted the machine guns so they could fire upward from the grounded helicopter—he could do nothing with the missiles.

But he had already decided. He had seen John and

Natalia fly sufficiently often that he felt he could get airborne. He couldn't maneuver enough to really fly and had no conception of how to land any sort of aircraft. But he could get the chopper airborne and into position to use the missiles. If he died—and he thought of Annie, perhaps dead already—if he died, she would find someone else—and he sniffed hard, realizing that tears were filling his eyes. It was insane, loving her, but he did. But saving her brother was more important than saving himself. Saving John's son—

And the twenty cryogenic sleep passengers and three crew members of Eden One. To save all of them was more important than one life when the one life was his.

He kept running toward the stolen Soviet helicopter through the rain—Eden One would be starting its approach soon, very soon.

* *

Chapter Fifty-Two

Natalia Anastasia Tiemerovna, fighting the nausea, fighting the sense of her own smell, banked the Soviet helicopter, following in the wake of Rourke's machine, Kurinami behind her as they convoyed the three ships toward what she prayed would be the final conflict with her husband. To intercept him at the least and prevent him from slaughtering Michael and Paul.

Sarah Rourke was strapped in beside her in the co-pilot's seat. "Do you remember what you shouted after John shot your husband?"

"I — I don't think — what?"

She looked at Sarah Rourke, envying the cleanness of her body in the instant.

"You shouted to John — you cried out, 'I love you' — that's what you said."

Natalia looked away from the instruments and into Sarah's green eyes. "Why were you and Annie and the others coming to rescue me?"

She watched Sarah Rourke as the wife of the man she loved laughed. "You came to rescue us, didn't you?"

"It — it was my fault — that Vladmir took you in the first place — all of this — "

"It wasn't your fault — stop blaming yourself. So you love my husband and your husband knows it. And so your husband's an animal. Your husband — he would have been the way he is without you or without John. The two of you, and us because of that—we're the focus of his hatred because we're here. So maybe I should hate you—because John loves you and you love him and because he let the children age so he could marry you off to Michael and bail himself out of a bad situation. Maybe I should love him because he wanted to give away the woman he loved just to avoid hurting me. I don't know—how I should feel, toward either of you. But whatever—there's nothing wrong with you except the guilt you keep heaping on yourself. And maybe I do the same thing—anyway. Well, anyway, we have something to do. And I would have come after you if the situation had been reversed—for what it's worth." Natalia suddenly realized she hadn't been looking at the controls and she turned away from Sarah. Sarah was still talking. "But as soon as we get on the ground, get into some clothes—you should see how ridiculous you look in Annie's slip and no shoes and John's leather jacket."

And Sarah Rourke started to laugh.

Natalia, feeling laughter welling up inside of her, whispered, "I feel ridiculous."

"What?"

"I feel ridiculous," she said louder, looking down at herself—her feet and legs were mud splattered. The slip clung to her thighs and the leather jacket was so big for her that she had rolled back the sleeves to her elbows so she could work the controls of the helicopter, and she let the laughter come now.

"Ridiculous—" Sarah was laughing and Natalia laughed with her.

Chapter Fifty-Three

"Coming out of Entry Interface communications blackout on my mark," Dodd sang out.

"My instruments check," Craig Lerner responded.

"Tiles cooling to acceptable level," Styles called.

"Mark!" As if he had hit a switch, static crackled over the radio and he could barely make out the voice of Paul Rubenstein coming over the radio. Dodd activated his microphone. "We're with you, Mr. Rubenstein." Dodd consulted his readouts. "Altitude thirty-four miles, air speed eight thousand two hundred-seventy plus and dropping at acceptable level. ETA to you twelve minutes. We are committed to your landing site. Talk to you later—Dodd out." Dodd studied the computer display screens on his control panel. "Switching to C.R.T.S. Craig—on my mark—"

"Ready to begin terminal area energy management," Styles called.

"Mark," Dodd called.

"On C.R.T.S., T.A.E.M. fully functional," Craig Lerner announced.

"Entry Flight Profile is good, skipper," Styles called out.

"Entry Flight Profile good," Dodd repeated. "Looking for Waypoint One."

"First gas tank on the left, skipper." Styles laughed.

"Thanks for that—making the S-Turn—"

"S-Turn looking good, skipper," Styles called."

"Making for Waypoint One," Lerner called out.

"C.R.T.S. looking good, skipper — time for a video game if we hurry."

"After we hit the ground." Dodd laughed.

"Don't use the word hit — say land." Lerner laughed.

"Coming up on Waypoint One," Dodd called out.

"Lookin' good on the C.R.T.S, T.A.E.M. right on the money, skipper."

"Roger that, Jeff," Dodd answered. "Ideal trajectory — so far."

"Keep encouraging me." Lerner laughed.

"Hitting Attitude Direction Indicator to correct for slight nose pitch."

"A.D.I. on the money, skipper."

"Horizontal Situation Indicator puts us right where we should be," Dodd said. "I need a roger on that, Jeff."

"Big affirmative on H.S.I. — looks just like a simulator flight."

"Will you guys cut it out — you know landings make me nervous," Lerner groused.

"Vertical Velocity Indicator okay to you, Jeff?"

"Roger that one, too, skipper — just like the stork's droppin' us — "

"Jees, guys," Lerner cut in.

Dodd studied the Alpha Mach Meter to the left of the A.D.I. and H.S.I. panels. "Arriving Waypoint One five minutes on my mark," Dodd called out, studying the C.R.T.S., the small box showing his position in the orbiter's immediate future. The box moved into the cylinder. "Mark — five minutes to Waypoint One."

"Boy, I'd better pack my toothbrush." Styles laughed.

"All right — be that way," Lerner groused again.

"Speed brake handle to sixty-five percent — moving now," Dodd called. Entering the cylinder, when he had done it on the simulators and the two times before that he had done it for real when landing one of the orbiters — although he had been committed from the moment he had made his altitudinal corrections to slow his orbiting speed, this always seemed like the ultimate commitment. No chance to play the controls and fly by the seat of the pants, no chance for anything but to bring her in and to land her. And his palms sweated now as he watched himself and his ship moving closer to the cylinder on the C.R.T. display. He thought of Craig Lerner, his flight officer, and said aloud, "Anybody got the instruction booklet — I think I forgot to do something a couple of minutes back."

Chapter Fifty-Four

Beside him in the side seat of the helicopter, Capt. Andre Popovski said, "Comrade Colonel—Eden One is estimated five minutes from touchdown on the landing field prepared for them along the highway."

Karamatsov shouted past Popovski to the pilot of the machine. "E.T.A. at the Rourke campsite—quickly!"

"Comrade colonel—almost exactly four minutes."

"Comrade colonel," Popovski interrupted. "Headquarters indicated the approach pattern should last eighty seconds after the space shuttle comes out of the turn and toward the landing zone for touchdown."

"Popovski—have the pilot plot an intercept course so we can follow the shuttle in—it will be like being in a shooting gallery. A popular thing once in America—did you ever try one, Popovski?"

"No, comrade colonel—I have—"

"Fascinating." Karamatsov raised an imaginary rifle to his shoulder, squinting along its imaginary barrel at its imaginary front sight, not really seeing the rain which came in torrents around the speeding helicopter, but seeing a tiny, two dimensional space shuttle, all in white, moving along a rail, with it ducks and tiny bull's-eyes, and tracking it with his eye. "Pow! Ha!" And he looked at Popovski. "Just like a shooting gallery, Popovski—and then, after the space shuttle is in flames and all aboard are dead, we strafe the Rourke campsite and we kill Michael Rourke and Rourke's Jew friend. And we fire our missiles into the highway surface and destroy it so the remaining craft of the Eden Project fleet cannot use the site for landing—ever. Perhaps they will be unable to land and simply die there in the cold of space, and someday the night sky will be bright as one by one the space shuttles lose their orbits and burn up on reentry into the atmosphere and the last of these fools who believed in democracy will all be dead. And we can hunt John Rourke and my wife and Rourke's wife and daughter and the other girl and the black woman with them and the Japanese—hunt them and destroy them."

Chapter Fifty-Five

John Rourke spoke into his headset radio, the set switched now to the frequency shared with the radio aboard Eden One. "This is John Rourke, captain — come in."

"Dr. Rourke — a little busy now — touchdown in just a little while. Over."

"I know as much about your touchdown schedule as you do — I'm flying one of the Soviet craft. I've been monitoring their communications — I'm sure Natalia and your Lieutenant Kurinami have been doing the same in their craft. There's a fleet of approximately eight Soviet gunships ready to interface with your descent pattern in approximately three minutes — just in time to shoot you down as you attempt to land. Can you do anything to change course and kill time until we can attempt to eliminate the threat? Over."

Rourke already knew the answer — no.

"You should be familiar with our procedures, Dr. Rourke — you already know the answer to that one, I'm sure. We have six M-16s stashed aboard and a hundred and eighty rounds of ammo for each, plus three .45 pistols with twenty-one rounds apiece. Can't open a window and shoot at them. Anyway, all of us are a little busy. Any chance they're bad shots, over?"

Rourke laughed at Dodd's remark despite the situation. "I wouldn't count on that, captain. We're moving into the area at maximum speed, burning fuel like a fifty-seven Chevy I bet, too, so hang in there and pray a little. Rourke out."

"God bless us all, doctor — Eden One out."

Rourke held to the same frequency "Rourke calling Paul — come in, Paul — Rourke calling Rubenstein — come in — over."

Static for a moment, then, "I've been monitoring you, John, and monitoring Eden One. I've got the gunship's machine guns set to fire against any attack force. And I've got something else up my sleeve if I have to. Michael's holding on. Dodd has the same blood type and the science officer can give a transfusion if he has to. Michael'll be okay. Over."

"Paul — get Michael into the Ford and drive out of there — the two of you will be sitting ducks on the ground. Over."

"How's Annie — and the others, too? Over."

"Annie's fine — and Sarah and Natalia and Madison and Halverson and Kurinami. But get out of there. Over."

"Negative, John. Michael's safe — he's too weak for me to move him. If I have to, I can get this crate airborne and use my missiles to defend Eden One. Over."

"Bullshit, Paul — you're not a pilot. Over."

"Anybody can get an aircraft off the ground and push a fire control switch. The hard part's landing it. I can see Eden One — hear her. Gotta go — tell Annie I do love her. Rubenstein out."

Rourke started to answer but Annie's voice came over the radio, from Kurinami's helicopter. "Paul — you'll only get yourself killed. Do as Daddy says — I love you — I don't want you to die."

Static.

Then Paul's voice. "If I make it, we'll connive Captain Dodd into marrying us. If I don't, then forget me. I love you—and I love all of you. Why the hell you think I'm doing this? Paul out."

Rourke almost shouted into the microphone. "Paul—do not attempt to fly that machine—Paul—I repeat—Paul!" He was shouting now. "Paul!"

There was nothing but static.

Rourke stared at the air speed indicator—the tachometer was almost redlining if he read it right. His voice almost a whisper now, Rourke said into his microphone. "Natalia—lieutenant—I'm gonna redline this thing—push for maximum speed—follow at present speed. If I blow this sucker up, at least your ships will still be functional. Rourke out." And Rourke flicked off the radio—he didn't want to hear Natalia and Sarah telling him not to do what he was going to do. He looked at Madison, telling the girl, "I'm sorry it's being like this—I mean—"

"Father Rourke—you love Paul Rubenstein very much—I would expect nothing less from you." Her pretty pale blue eyes seemed to smile at him and Rourke reached across to her and squeezed both her hands. Then he released her hands and let the throttle all the way out. And he prayed.

Chapter Fifty-Six

Paul Rubenstein followed the Eden One Communications—they had begun something called autoland guidance—he wished he had it as he fired the engine of the Soviet helicopter, his hands trembling as he strapped himself into the pilot's seat. "Pilot's seat." He laughed aloud. "Wrong place for me." He laughed again.

Two M-16s and spare magazines, though he doubted there'd be time to use the spares at any event. The Schmeisser. The battered Browning High Power, the first gun he had ever "owned"—the High Power was in the tanker holster across his chest. After he fired the full compliment of missiles, he would go to the machine guns—he had locked them again into their mounts. Then the M-16s, then the Schmeisser and the High Power. Until the machine crashed or until he had no more ammunition for the guns, he would keep fighting, whichever came first—he would keep fighting.

Even if John and Natalia and Lieutenant Kurinami arrived in time with their gunships, they would be outnumbered by at least more than two to one.

Perhaps. Perhaps he could make a difference, Paul Rubenstein told himself. He reached up to the bridge of his nose for his glasses—but they weren't there. Since awakening from the cryogenic sleep, he had had no need for the glasses. But a lifetime of habit was hard to break.

But he was about to break all habits. He smiled. Once and forever.

He looked to his left, toward the tent on the far side of the campsite well away from the road—he closed his eyes and prayed that Michael would live. Before the Night of The War, he had found every excuse not to go to Temple. Since the Night of The War, he had often wished there still were a Temple to go to. He thought of his father and his mother, how it had been on the holidays—the first time he had been allowed to light the candles.

He felt the tears in his eyes, wiped them away from his eyes with the back of his right hand so he could see, then found the throttle—the machine lurched, pitching forward, and he tried to keep his hands steady as gradually, the machine began to rise.

In the distance, to his right as the machine spun for a moment, he could see the shape of Eden One, starting its final approach—he had watched the space shuttles, one or another of them, land ever since the very first landing. It had always fascinated him, filled him with awe, made him stop to offer a silent prayer for the safety of the crew.

He murmured the same prayer now.

And then he looked to his left.

Eight black shapes like giant wasps, shapes identical to the shape which housed him.

The Soviet gunship force, Vladmir Karamatsov in the lead. He knew somehow that Karamatsov would not miss it.

Slowly, Paul Rubenstein worked the controls, try-

195

ing to determine what was what.

Slowly, the machine turned to face the oncoming gunships.

He worked the switch to arm the missiles, the targeting computer display appearing on the console. "All right, asshole," he told the eight enemy gunships and the man who had brought them. "Come ahead."

His hands had stopped trembling — he was ready to die now.

Chapter Fifty-Seven

The helicopter vibrated around them, Madison — her voice remarkably calm sounding — saying, "I think this flying machine is about to fall to pieces, Father Rourke!"

Rourke didn't look at her, studying the eight black shapes on the far horizon instead. "If she hasn't already, she won't now — I hope."

"Why is a flying machine called like a woman?"

"Vehicles are temperamental, sometimes unpredictable — like a woman."

"I was always taught to be even tempered, to control excesses."

"Well, there's a fallacy there — men are just as temperamental, just as unpredictable, except that men mask their emotions more than women do. Calling an aircraft by a woman's name is just an outgrowth of a more chauvinistic era."

"What is shaw — shaw — "

"Chauvinistic — c-h-a-u-v-i-n-i-s-t-i-c — like assuming women always need help with things, protecting women, the man taking the responsibility — "

"You are — show — one of these?"

Rourke looked at her and smiled. "How could you tell?"

And the girl laughed.

Rourke set his attention to the growing shapes on

the horizon, and farther distant now—he could see Eden One—just barely through the pouring rain. Its speed he judged at less than five hundred miles per hour—perhaps two minutes before touchdown. The eight black gunship shapes were spreading into some sort of attack formation.

John Rourke punched up his weapons systems consoles, saying to Madison though not looking at her, "Keep that M-16 handy and the other ones, too." She had them beside her in the copilot's chair. "When we get into this, you can ram one of those out the storm vent beside you—the brass'll go into the back of the ship and shouldn't hit the control panels. We'll need all the firepower we can get. Aim for the rotors—the blades on top of the machines, or for the open side doors—you can get some of the personnel aboard maybe. I'll be moving fast—so watch you don't bump your head on the glass. If a missile hits us, we'll be dead in just a couple of seconds anyway, so don't worry."

"No, Father Rourke—I will not worry."

Rourke picked one chopper as his immediate target and altered course to intersect it.

What worried him most was the solitary helicopter which hovered somehow strangely near the roadside that was to be the runway—and he knew the pilot, knew him like his brother.

Chapter Fifty-Eight

The eight enemy helicopters had broken into what Paul Rubenstein recognized as an attack formation—and there was a ninth helicopter, some distance further back closing fast.

It would be John Rourke—but John Rourke would be too late unless he—Paul Rubenstein—acted to break up the formation.

Paul Rubenstein settled the attack computer on the nearest of the gunships, the sound of Eden One coming in, the sound of the gunships almost nonexistent.

He activated the fire control switch for the primary starboard missiles, the entire compliment aboard, the tubes reloaded after John Rourke had used the missiles to destroy the bridges. The contrail snaked away from his ship, Paul feeling the ship shudder as it hovered over the sand—it seemed to him like miles over the sand as he looked downward for an instant.

His eyes flickered back to the contrail—the lead chopper seemed to stall in midair, then bits and pieces of it were flying everywhere, a huge black and orange fireball encircling the gunship, shrouding it, the gunship gone from sight.

There was a contrail coming toward him—Paul Rubenstein fired again. The missiles crossed, he guessed, less than a dozen yards from each other.

His own ship shuddered, the missile missing by

inches and Paul Rubenstein laughed. They had not counted on him to keep the aircraft entirely stationary, being unable to actually fly it.

The second missile he had fired connected, another of the gunships a ball of yellow and orange flame.

He made to fire a third missile, the sound to starboard deafening as he glanced toward it. One of the gunships, machine guns blazing. Paul Rubenstein tried to turn his machine as the machine guns opened up, the plexiglass of the dome shattering around him, fire burning inside him as he doubled forward, his right fist locked on the aircraft's throttle, his left hand trying to find the fire control switch to mass fire the remaining missiles — he found it, depressed the switch, the helicopter shuddering maddeningly, the sound of the massive launch deafening him as he screamed with the pain burning in his chest and abdomen.

Blackness — cold and numbing — he shouted one word. "Annie!"

Chapter Fifty-Nine

John Rourke fired port and starboard missiles, one each, both missiles targeted on the gunship that had fired on Paul Rubenstein, Rubenstein's craft still airborne somehow, the plexiglass cockpit bubble shattered, smoke billowing from the fuselage. "Fuck you!" He screamed the words into the teardrop-shaped microphone before his lips, the radio set to the Russian frequency.

As the contrails wove toward the target, the gunships started to turn, Rourke heard Karamatsov's voice. "That was the little Jew?"

An explosion, then a second explosion, the gunship which had fired on Paul Rubenstein vaporizing, the fireball consuming it, then dissipating on the wind as another of the black gunships banked sharply and suddenly away from it. The rain was so heavy now the wipers in front of the cockpit did virtually no good, the defrosters at full power but the interior of the plexiglass steaming over.

"Madison—take a rag or something and wipe the windshield for me—the glass—so I can see," Rourke commanded, swinging the helicopter one hundred eighty degrees to starboard, Rubenstein's machine still airborne. Rourke switched frequencies, to the shuttle frequency—Paul's radio would be set to it. "Paul—come in, Paul!"

There was no answer.

"Paul!"

Static, then Natalia's voice. "He must be dead, John — I am sorry."

"Get in here — you and Kurinami — we're getting those bastards — now!" Rourke worked the missiles' control switch again, discharging one of the starboard missiles, the shot a miss, the missile disappearing into the rain.

He glanced to his left — Eden One was coming in, approaching the runway surface, two of the remaining five gunships broken off, starting an attack run. Rourke spoke into the radio as he banked the machine toward them. "Natalia — you and Kurinami go after the other three — get them. I'm going in after the two that broke off."

Rourke turned to glance at Madison for a moment. "Hang on, kid." He throttled out, starting down after the two gunships.

"I am hanging on, Father Rourke!"

He didn't answer her — the space shuttle had deployed landing gear. "Shit," Rourke snarled, edging the throttle out still more, the two gunships dogging the shuttle craft now, one on each side.

A missile contrail — but a miss, the ground to the far starboard side of the Eden One craft erupting with the explosion, the rain streaming down, the dirt and sand as well now as Rourke leveled off, not risking his missiles, the gunship's machine gun armed.

He was flying over the shuttle craft now, the superior speed of the shuttle sucking him along in its wake, Rourke firing his machine guns toward the enemy gunship to port.

The contrail of a missile again, Rourke firing the machine guns, his fire pattern crossing the streaking missiles, the missiles exploding in midair, Rourke's gunship punching through the cloud of smoke and flame, the plexiglass of the cockpit bubble scorching black with it, the rain forming clouds of steam around him, Rourke throttling out, the space shuttle starting to touch down. Above the roar of his guns, he could hear the skidding of the tires as they touched the wet surface, the Eden One craft vibrating, twisting beneath him, more machine gun fire pouring from both helicopters now. Rourke chanced it, banking slightly, throttling back, cutting forty-five degrees to starboard, firing his portside missiles in cluster, the enemy gunship dogging the shuttle craft's starboard side vaporizing, the roar of the multiple warhead impacts deafening as Rourke banked to port, climbing now, the second gunship firing another missile, a chunk of the road surface in the wake of Eden One exploding, particles of concrete and rock debris pelting at Rourke's gunship as he still climbed, then brought his nose down to attack the attacker.

Another contrail from the enemy gunship — a miss, the missile impacting at the side of the road, the shuttle craft slowing now, less than two hundred miles per hour as it skidded insanely along the wet road surface.

"Hold on, Madison," Rourke rasped, the girl leaning back, the windshield wiped clean of steam. He could hear her M-16 firing through the copilot's side storm window, firing at the last gunship he knew. "Hang on." Rourke cut off his fire control computer, the machine guns on manual now, the distance between the enemy gunship and the slowing Eden One too slight now to risk a missile.

There was a voice in Russian coming over the headset — he had switched back to their frequency. "Should we break off, comrade colonel — the American pursues us, over." There was no answer for a moment, then a low, almost whispered reply. "This is Colonel Karamatsov — destroy Eden One or answer to me."

Rourke punched the microphone control. "Rourke to Karamatsov — bite my ass!" Rourke touched the machine gun fire control switch, port and starboard guns firing, the distance between Rourke's ship and the enemy gunship yards now only, the wash of the rotor blades surging rain water against Rourke's cockpit bubble faster than the wiper blades could work to remove it, the machine gun fire lacing into the enemy ship's cockpit bubble, across the rotor, crisscrossing the tail rotor, the enemy gunship starting to move erratically now, veering to port.

Rourke moved his fingers to the missile control switch, firing — one starboard missile, the contrail almost lost in the sheets of rain, the contrail vanishing then, in the next instant the Soviet gunship a huge black and orange fireball rolling over and over and over, chunks of the gunship spraying along the road surface in the wake of the Eden One craft, Rourke hitting the frequency controls to contact Eden One. "Hang in there, guys — I got 'em off your back. Rourke out." Rourke banked the gunship hard to starboard, crossing over Eden One's dorsal side, turning the craft ninety degrees, leveling off, closing toward the last three gunships — Natalia's and Kurinami's crafts were exchanging missiles with them, all five craft using evasive maneuvers, the missiles impacting the desert sands beneath them.

Rourke switched back to the Soviet frequency. Karamatsov's voice—". . . must provide covering fire. You will be remembered, you will be avenged!"

One of the three enemy gunships broke off, heading southeast, another of the gunships exploding as Natalia's craft—Rourke had memorized the respective serial numbers of Natalia's and Kurinami's gunships to avoid confusion in battle—veered away, one of Natalia's missiles having impacted.

Rourke activated his remaining starboard missiles, Kurinami's machine guns firing, Natalia's machine guns opening up as well now, the cockpit bubble of the enemy gunship disintegrating, flames leaping skyward, the body of a man—a human torch—vaulting through the flames into midair.

Rourke's missiles impacted, the helicopter gunship exploding, the body of the burning airborne man consumed in the larger fireball of the exploding gunship.

Rourke banked hard to starboard, Karamatsov's gunship disappearing over the horizon, the rain as heavy as it had been. That it could fall more heavily seemed impossible as Rourke stared after Karamatsov.

Rourke glanced to his right—Eden One had stopped.

He glanced to his left—the tent where he had left Michael at the far edge of the campsite and away from the road—it looked untouched.

And then Rourke turned the aircraft one hundred eighty degrees—somehow, Paul Rubenstein's crippled gunship still hovered over the desert, perhaps eight hundred feet up.

Rourke switched to the common frequency with Natalia's and Kurinami's crafts. "Natalia—you know how to give a transfusion—so does Sarah. Touch down and start Michael with Sarah's blood. As soon as Annie reaches you connect her so you can switch to her when Sarah's through. Over."

"What about—about—"

The static.

Rourke spoke into his microphone. "I said I'll get him and I will—take care of Michael. Have Kurinami meet when I land—hurry. Out." Rourke started the machine down. "Madison—find me a grappling hook if this thing has one."

"A what?"

"A big three-pronged hook on the end of a rope—"

"I have seen such a thing—it is put away back there."

"Stowed—you say stowed—get it. Quick—when I touch down, get out and get Kurinami aboard."

"You are going to try to save Mr. Rubenstein."

Rourke looked at her, then realized the stub of cigar in his mouth was chewed to where it was shredded. He tossed it through the storm vent. "Yeah—I am." Rourke started checking his controls to land. "I am," he repeated.

Chapter Sixty

Rourke idled the engine, leaving the cockpit to the midsection of the fuselage, staring out into the rain for a moment through the partially open fuselage door, watching as Madison ran toward Kurinami's landing craft, the ground turned to oozing mud, the rain lashing at the ground and at the gunships. Rourke dropped to a crouch, checking the grappling hook's connection to the rope, mentally gauging the length of the rope as he began constructing the knot.

He stood, peering out into the rain again, Kurinami talking to Madison.

Rourke undid his gunbelt from his waist, stowing it under one of the seats. His shoulder holsters — he slipped these off, placing them beside his musette bag and his binoculars, then stowing them with the Python's gunbelt. The Detonics Scoremasters — he pulled these from his belt and set them away. From the musette bag, he took a spare pair of boot laces.

The little A.G. Russell Sting IA Black Chrome. He set this down as well. He took the gunbelt in his hands, unthreaded the holster, the ammo carriers, then the knife sheath. Rourke began threading the big Gerber MkII to his trouser belt. It would be all that he needed.

Kurinami — looking up, Rourke could see the Japanese naval aviator running toward Rourke's craft. The Japanese bounded up, aboard, slamming the fuselage door along its tracks and locking it.

"Madison says that you require my assistance, doctor."

"You're a good pilot and I don't need your blood type. Yeah — we're takin' this crate up to as close as we can get to Paul Rubenstein in that helicopter just hovering out there."

"It is on fire — it will explode at any moment."

"Electrical fire — could take a long time."

Kurinami's eyes — Rourke followed them to the grappling hook. "You wish — "

"You got it. I get this grappling hook attached, then I climb over to Paul's machine and I get aboard. I get Paul, attach both of us to the end of the rope with the grappling hook, then I cut us free and you take her straight up to kill the pendulum motion. As soon as everybody's clear, use the machine guns and go for Paul's main rotor and blow the ship out of the sky before it drifts over Eden One or over the campsite. Simple, right?" Rourke didn't wait for an answer, starting forward. "You take the pilot's controls, I'll ride copilot until we get into position."

"But — but Dr. Rourke — your friend — he is probably already dead."

Rourke started strapping himself into the copilot's seat. "If he is, I'll bring his body back. Out of all the people on Eden Project Shuttles, well — I know for fact some of them were Israeli. And that means they're Jewish — at least Paul can have a decent burial. Come on — you said yourself, the ship could explode any minute." Rourke started airborne as Kurinami eased into the pilot's seat and began strapping in.

Chapter Sixty-One

The radius of a single main rotor blade for the Soviet gunships Rourke had judged as being thirty-six and one-half feet. Twice that radius—the ship Kurinami piloted and the ship which smoked and burned and carried Paul Rubenstein—dead? Twice that radius plus approximately twelve more feet. One of the seatbelts strung out and threaded around Rourke's waist, John Rourke leaned away from the fuselage, his feet braced on the runner, the rope coiled in his left hand, the end with the grappling hook in his right as he fed out the hook more and more, the other end of the rope secured to the runner beneath Rourke's feet.

To swing the hook was easy enough, but to swing it while keeping it sufficiently low that it would not foul in the rotor blades flashing over his head was the trick, he knew. Rain pelted him in torrents, forced against his body in the rotor downdraft, his eyes squinted almost shut against it as he swung the grappling hook outward.

A miss.

He began coiling in the rope, his headset microphone buzzing in his ear. "Doctor—you can never get enough swing to the hook this way. I have a plan. It is very dangerous but when considered, little more dangerous than our current endeavors."

"Shoot," Rourke rasped into the teardrop microphone, rainwater rushing down his face, filling his mouth as he spit it away.

"I will fly our own craft beneath that of the unfortunate Mr. Rubenstein. As I pass beneath, I will bank sharply to starboard. Your body will be pressed back against the fuselage. You can throw the grappling hook almost straight upward if we time the maneuver perfectly. You will have one chance—and I do not know if I will be able to get the craft we ride righted again. Do you wish to make the attempt?"

"Try it—talk me through as you start to bank. Good luck."

"*Hai—go seiko wo inorimasu!*"

Rourke felt his face seam with a smile as he coiled in the grappling hook end of the rope, waiting, ready.

Kurinami had dry run it once—but nothing was dry, the rain unceasing. Kurinami had piloted the gunship in a gradual circle over Paul's ship, then beneath it and coming out and climbing to a level position with the ship again.

"I am ready, doctor—if you're ready."

"Best pilot in the Japanese navy, right?"

"Helicopters were not my specialty."

"Thanks—let's go—just remember—there's not that much extra rope. After we hook up, you can't get beyond one hundred and fifty feet or you'll snap the rope or make both ships crash."

"I am aware of this—hey—dark of the moon, huh?"

"You bet—let's go." Rourke swung the grappling hook in his right hand, the helicopter beginning the upward portion of the arc. Rourke spoke into the microphone again. "Looking good, lieutenant."

"Thank you, doctor—I thought so myself."

They were directly above Paul's gunship now, the

smoke billowing from the open fuselage door darker now and more of it, bright tongues of orange flame visible licking up in the cockpit. Rourke could see Paul Rubenstein, slumped forward over the controls now.

Rourke shifted the hook end of the rope to his left hand and crossed himself with his right.

He took the rope back again in his right hand. Kurinami was over Rubenstein's ship and beyond it now, starting to descend, starting to pick up speed as he banked the ship hard to port, Rourke sagging away from the fuselage, the pressure of the seatbelt cutting into his abdomen. The knuckles of his right hand were beginning to spurt blood again, some of the scabs there washed away.

The helicopter veered to starboard, Rourke bracing himself as best he could as his body slammed back against the fuselage, the pressure of the seatbelt gone, his head swimming suddenly with dizziness. He fought it, the helicopter to which he was attached starting to bank as it crossed beneath Rubenstein's ship. "Now, doctor—now."

Rourke was already swinging the grappling hook, the force of the thing ripping at his bare right hand, the blood spurting from his knuckles even more rapidly now as he swung the grappling hook over his head, toward the runner beneath Rubenstein's gunship.

He could see the hook—as if everything around him moved in slow motion, the hook smashing against the fuselage undercarriage, falling, one of the three hook blades catching, starting to pull away, then hooking over the runner, Rourke's right arm almost jerked from its socket, the rope burning his flesh as it played out through his fingers, Rourke letting the rope out coils at a time now as the helicopter's engine stuttered. "Doctor—the craft is not responding."

"Make it respond — we're connected."

"I must increase air speed — if I cannot bring us out of it any other way, you must cut the rope."

"Bullshit," Rourke rasped into the headset microphone, the sound of Kurinami's engine still uneven, the craft lurching wildly, still banked hard to starboard. There was a sputtering — the rotor beat higher pitched now — the rain pelting at Rourke's face and hands more strongly, the chopper starting to rise, all of the rope played out from Rourke's left hand, starting to go taut.

"Hold on!" Kurinami's voice.

The chopper leveled off, hovered. "We are both lucky men, doctor," Kurinami's voice echoed in Rourke's ear.

"Skill — that's all it ever is," Rourke told him, reaching to his hip pocket for his gloves. "I'm ditching the headset now and starting across. If the ship Paul's on looks like it's about to go, I'll cut the line and you get the hell out."

"I will stay, thank you — it is a borrowed aircraft anyway — but hurry!"

"Right." Rourke ripped the headset away, throwing it behind him into the fuselage.

Slowly, Rourke lowered his body into a crouch, leaning toward the rope which was the umbilical cord from one craft to another.

Rourke's right fist closed over the rope, the knuckle area of his gloves dark with wetness — either the blood from the reopened cuts on his knuckles or the rain — he told himself it was the rain.

His left hand moved to the buckle of the seat belt and Rourke popped it, half lurching downward, his left fist closing over the rope as well, his right leg hooking over the rope behind his knee.

His left leg swung free and Rourke pulled with his

hands and his right leg, getting his left leg up and over the rope.

He looked down. "Oh, shit," he snarled, the drop at least eight hundred feet, and as he looked up, the downdraft of the rotor blades washed his eyes with rain. He squinted his eyes shut tight against it, no way to wipe the water away.

He opened his eyes, edging his left hand forward, then his right, his knees pressed tight around the rope as he inched ahead, hand over hand, the rope vibrating maddeningly, taut one moment, slack the next, the rain hammering down at him, his gloves saturated with it now.

John Rourke craned his neck to look ahead—more than one hundred feet remained until he reached the stricken helicopter and his friend. He kept moving, hand over hand, the interior of his gloves wet now, his body shivering with the cold rain and the feeling of being suspended on a thread over the abyss which led to the rain-soaked ground eight hundred feet below.

Rourke kept going, hand over hand. He forced his mind away from what he did, his hands aching, his arms stiffening under the strain, his legs cramping. "Paul—I'll be there—on my way, Paul—hang on. Don't move and touch those controls—I'm coming—hang on."

Rourke closed his eyes against the rain—he saw Natalia's face—the terror that had been there, the blueness of her eyes, the horror they had seen. Karamatsov. "Karamatsov," Rourke hissed into the rain, drawing himself onward. He would follow Vladmir Karamatsov, to Russia if that was where Karamatsov had gone, to the ends of the Earth if that was where—to kill him for once and for all and forever this time.

"Paul!" Rourke shouted the word, feeling the surge of

anger. That Natalia had been so abused and degraded, that Michael had been shot and perhaps even now was dying, that Paul had willingly sacrificed and might now even be dead — It was not hatred, Rourke knew — because hatred wasted energy, denied thinking. It was the need to exterminate something unspeakably vile.

One hand forward, then another. Again. Right, left, his arms past aching now, his hands stiff, the fingers unmoving as he forced his body along the rope.

John Rourke looked toward Rubenstein's gunship — less than twenty feet remained.

The right fist. The left fist. Drag the legs. The right fist. The left fist. Drag the legs. The right fist. The left fist. Drag the legs.

Ten feet.

Rourke kept moving. Right, left, right, left, right — his left hand felt something hard, the huge knot, actually six knots in one. Eight inches past this knot he could see the runner. One thrust and he was there.

Rourke squinted his eyes against the rain to look at it, the rain somehow more intense — the downdraft from Paul's rotors.

Rourke hooked his right wrist over the runner, then his left, clamping both hands together, resting the fingers, hanging from the rope only by his legs.

His elbows — he hooked one, then the other over the runner, sagging down from it, drawing breath into his body, telling his fingers and hands to respond.

Movement — his right hand moved along the length of the runner, the fingers closing over it, his muscles screaming at his brain to stop the insanity.

His left hand — he closed his fingers over the runner. He threw his body from the rope, his right hand shifting along the length of the runner, his left holding on, his right leg free of the rope, swinging wildly in the air, his left leg groping, hooking over the after end of the runner.

Smoke billowed around him—he was near the fuselage door.

Rourke looked up—insulation was burning. He could smell it.

His left hand—Rourke reached for the lip of the fuselage door, closing over it, his right leg swung up over the runner now.

Rourke's right hand braced now against the fuselage door at the side, and he twisted his right leg beneath him, bracing his right foot against the runner, thrusting himself forward, falling through the billowing grey smoke and into the helicopter.

His eyes streamed water—but tears from the smoke now, flames crackling around him, sparks rising, flickering, dying, the smell of gasoline heavy on the air.

Rourke pulled himself to his knees, staggering to his feet, lurching forward. "Paul!"

Rourke dropped to his knees beside the pilot's seat, Paul Rubenstein's face grey, drawn, blood trickling from the right corner of his mouth. Rourke gently eased the younger man back, Rourke's right hand grasping the controls—Paul's body had braced the controls. Only the slightest movement would have thrown the helicopter wildly out of control.

Rourke found the autopilot switch, tracing beneath it that the wiring was not aflame from the console. He hit the switch, the helicopter lurching once, the rotor sound shifting, uneven, then even again.

Rourke pushed himself up, quickly feeling for a pulse—a weak one in Rubenstein's neck.

215

Rourke explored Rubenstein's chest and abdomen.

Abdominal wounds. A chest wound—both lungs seemed inflated as best Rourke could tell.

A wound, bleeding heavily, in the right side of the neck — Rourke reached into his pocket and found his bandana. He packed the bandana against Rubenstein's neck, pulling the harness for the tanker holster up to secure it there.

"We gotta get out of here, Paul." Rourke withdrew the Gerber from its sheath, cutting Rubenstein free of the seat harness, cutting the harness free at the base where the straps exited the seat itself. He could use it. Rourke turned to the copilot's seat as he bent forward, water streaming from his hair and across his face. He cut away the harness here as well.

Crisscrossing the straps, he made a larger harness out of the two, fixing it around his back, eyeballing it for size, nodding to himself. He started aft, to the passenger compartment, cutting away seat belt harness there as well, adding these pieces into the sling he was building.

The pilot and copilot seat restraints formed natural loops interconnected as they were, Rourke starting forward again now. He dropped down beside Paul, the smoke more dense, tongues of flame licking upward from the wiring, because the control consoles—in seconds, perhaps, all control for the ship would be gone, including the autopilot.

Rourke eased Paul up into his arms, letting the bloodied chest sag against his own, sliding the harness beneath his friend, then letting Paul down again. Rourke gently moved Paul's legs, passing them through the loops of the harness one at a time. Paul groaned, his eyes opening. "John? Are—are you dead—dead, too?"

"Neither one of us is dead yet, Paul—just hang in there. We'll be safe in a minute here."

"You can't be—" His eyes closed as Rourke secured the harness. Paul's eyes opened again. "I didn't mean it to be like—but I did what—"

"Without what you did, Michael'd be dead and Eden One would have been destroyed. You're the hero of the day—but I got to get you out of here—rest easy, old friend." Paul Rubenstein nodded his head once and his eyes closed—Rourke checked for a pulse. It was somehow slightly stronger.

Rourke nodded to his friend. "Rest easy—Annie's waiting for you." Rourke raised to his full height, his head almost bumping the cabin ceiling as he shifted his own arms into the harness.

Rourke doubled forward, his back on fire with pain as he dragged Rubenstein from the pilot's seat and across his own body. Rourke secured the harness, square knotting the severed ends at his abdomen and at his chest.

Bearing his own weight and the weight of his friend, Rourke stumbled aft, the smoke denser still, flames now licking from the fuselage walls at Rourke's arms and legs.

The fuselage door. Rourke reached it, Rubenstein's Schmeisser banging against Rourke's rib cage. He started to take the Gerber to the sling—but Paul and the Schmeisser—the MP-40—they somehow went together.

Rourke left the subgun where it was.

Rourke reached into his left front Levi's pocket—the spare pair of boot laces from his musette bag. Quickly, he knotted the four ends together, doubling the thickness.

Rourke edged toward the fuselage doorway, slowly, carefully, placing his right foot out onto the runner, the helicopter shifting slightly under the combined weight, almost imperceptibly so.

His left foot now, his hands all that held him, braced against the fuselage door frame.

He stood on the runner, edging aft, holding to the fuselage, the rain ripping at his face, his hair, drenching him to the skin, freezing him.

The grappling hook. Rourke bent toward it, his left hand only all that held them now, his feet balanced precariously on the rain-slicked runner.

The boot laces. He looped the double laces over the massive knot eight inches away from the hook on the other side of the hook, away from the gunship. He doubled the laces through themselves, one loop cinched over the massive knot, the other in his right hand.

Rourke edged his right foot forward, passing his boot into the loop.

He would have one chance.

The Gerber—he looped the thong in the drilled-through handle over his left wrist, the thong caught against the bezel of his Rolex Submariner. His right hand gripped the rope, his body weight and Paul's leaned against the fuselage, both feet on the runners.

He shifted his shoulders under Paul's weight, hoping Kurinami was watching.

The rope would drag him from the crippled gunship—but he'd need more than that.

Rourke extended his right hand as far along the rope as he could reach, tiny explosions starting in the aircraft now, the smoke more intense, heat something he could feel through the fuselage walls.

Rourke closed his eyes, summoning his energy. One last thing to do.

His left arm arced downward, the saw teeth of the Gerber biting hard against the rope just above the grappling hook, the rope snapping taut, then going slack. His left hand moved back and forth, back and forth, sawing at the rope. One strand gone. The second gone, the rope going taut. Rourke hacked at it once, letting go of the knife as the rope snapped, throwing his body weight outward, his left hand groping for the rope as the rope dragged him from the fuselage, his right shoulder feeling for the second time as though it were ripping from the socket.

The Gerber swung on its wrist thong, Rourke's left hand finding the rope as they swung in free space, downward, falling like stones, Rubenstein's weight suddenly gone as their motion compensated for it. Rourke felt as though he were flying, his right leg stiffening as he clutched both hands to the rope now. His right boot braced against the boot lace stirrup he had made, the stirrup supported against the massive knot.

Swinging—weightless.

Suddenly Rourke's body lurched, his stomach churning, his neck snapping back, his arms aching, his back aching as Rubenstein's weight returned to him.

Rourke squinted upward against the rain—Kurinami's chopper was climbing, the wind rushing around Rourke like a scream.

Gunfire—he could barely hear it.

He looked to his left, the wind tearing at him—Paul Rubenstein's pirated gunship exploded in midair as machine gun fire from Kurinami's ship etched its way across the fuselage.

Rourke turned his face away—but he didn't close his eyes, not daring to.

Chapter Sixty-Two

John Rourke sagged to his knees, then fell flat into the mud, Natalia kneeling in the mud beside him, Sarah raising his head in her hands.

And suddenly the weight was gone and an unfamiliar voice was shouting, "We're clear, lieutenant." But the voice *was* familiar.

John Rourke rolled over onto his back, Natalia pulling his gloves from his hands, holding his hands to her face, kissing them, Sarah Rourke cradling his head in her lap.

"You're Dodd," Rourke rasped, staring at a tall, prematurely grey man dressed in sodden, once white coveralls.

"I bet after all that you're even glad to see me — Dr. Rourke. I'd offer to shake hands but your hands don't look too good right now."

"Michael — how's —"

Sarah answered. "Mr. Styles says Michael should make it — they've already begun the cryogenic awakening for the doctor they had on board — they began it when they touched down. And Annie and I both gave him blood."

"Didn't have much to lose, doctor — but our doctor'll be on the job."

"Paul — he needs —"

It was Styles, Rourke guessed. "You can tell me what to do — use my hands — we can stabilize Mr. Rubenstein until our doctor is up and around."

"When I was in Viet Nam," Dodd said and grinned,

rain still pouring down. "Well—I saw men shot up worse and live. I'll bet you have, too."

Rourke only nodded, Natalia and Sarah flanking him now, helping him to sit up, his back muscles tightening—but he could still breathe. He could see Paul now, Annie caressing his face, supporting his head as Elaine Halverson and Madison and another of the astronauts—Rourke guessed Flight Officer Lerner—eased him onto a blanket stretcher.

"Excuse me—gotta check our patient." Styles grinned.

Rourke sat up more. "I'll be all right," he told his wife and Natalia. "Have Kurinami keep one of the choppers ready to go airborne. The two of you," he said and looked at Sarah and then at Natalia, "organize some sort of defensive posture for the camp. We still have those Nazis and their gunships north of us somewhere—and there could be some stragglers from Karamatsov's force passing this way."

Rourke started to his feet.

"Wait a minute," Sarah whispered, and she reached out her right hand and held Natalia's right hand, and she bent her face toward him and kissed Rourke's mouth hard once. "For a while—well—I forgot the one thing I always did love about you, and always will no matter how the three of us work out. What you did for Paul—well—it reminded me." She got to her feet, picked up an M-16 and started running through the rain toward Kurinami's helicopter as it started to touch down.

Chapter Sixty-Three

Wolfgang Mann belted his trench coat about his waist and pulled his cap low over his forehead, then jumped from the fuselage door of his gunship into the mud in which he had landed.

He recognized the Third Corps haupsturm führer as the man ran across the mud-soaked field toward him. "Weil—your report," and Mann cupped his gloved hands around the flame of his lighter as he fired his cigarette— he had tasted a sample of the tobacco that had been grown under lights once and it had been very bad. But the crops grown outside the complex yielded a satisfying smoke, and complex scientists had fifty years ago found a method to remove all possible carcinogens. He had known nothing better, he reflected.

"All of the Soviet personnel who escaped on the ground have been accounted for, Herr Standarten Führer." He saluted.

Mann nodded. "Prisoners?"

"No, Herr Standarten Führer. Three of the Soviets committed suicide, regrettably."

"And what of the others. The ones who left the field?"

"The Soviet gunships were tracked, Herr Standarten Führer. There was a battle—and also—but it seems impossible."

"What, Weil?"

"One of the space shuttle craft read about in the history

222

books, those utilized by the Americans before the war between the superpowers—it—it landed, Herr Standarten Führer."

Mann inhaled on the cigarette—it was already wet. "Take no action—keep the area under surveillance but do not alert any personnel in the area to our presence. That is understood?"

"Yes, Herr Standarten Führer!" And the haupsturm führer raised his hand in salute, Mann again only nodding as the man turned on his heels and ran off across the field.

Wolfgang Mann studied the glowing tip of his cigarette, rain pouring down from his cap brim, his trouser legs beneath the protection of the trench coat already soaked.

A space shuttle. Americans still alive and fighting Russians. And the Russians themselves.

The key, he reflected, walking back toward his helicopter to get in out of the rain, would be to somehow turn these diverse elements to his advantage. To occupy the First and Second Corps with the pursuit of the Russians, and then to form some sort of alliance perhaps with the Americans.

Wolfgang Mann recalled the words of the British Prime Minister Sir Winston Churchill—and he laughed. Mann's own ancestor had been one of the highest ranking members of the SS to survive the Second World War. But Churchill—he recalled the words as best he could remember them. He had been more smitten with the mistakes of history than its aphorisms. Something about making an alliance with the devil himself to defeat Hitler.

Mann shrugged as he climbed back into his attack helicopter, snapping the cigarette butt into the rain to die. He too—Mann—would make an alliance to defeat Hitler's more than two dozen generations-removed successor. With the devil, or with the men who believed in freedom as did he.

He stood in the doorway and watched the rain fall for some time.